Recollections
of
Infidelity

Recollections
of
Infidelity

NINA LOURIK

Ivy House
Publishing Group

www.ivyhousebooks.com

PUBLISHED BY IVY HOUSE PUBLISHING GROUP
5122 Bur Oak Circle, Raleigh, NC 27612
United States of America
919-782-0281
www.ivyhousebooks.com

ISBN: 1-57197-445-8
Library of Congress Control Number: 2005901093

Printed in the United States of America

Remenbering my mother saying, "That's life."

Preface

Adulthood introduces us to words of profanity and sexual awareness as written here—much to my disdain with reality as it exists.

The words in this story begin in a place referred to as Sin City rather than its rightful name, when at one time notoriously known for its whores, pimps, deceit, exploitation, and numerous taverns. After eight years of employment in a motel located in the heart of this city, the author relates a web of experiences during those years revealing situations commanding one to wonder—"What next?"

The stories do not end here. They continue into the adversity of many in pursuit of a dream for happiness with their special first love, including the author's very own family. Two sisters vehemently and threateningly objected to these writings. Are you curious?

Chapter One

The Phantom Motel

Tom Stevens was a handsome salesman with a mammoth ego who patronized the Southtown Motel. He was regarded as a perfect gentleman, husband, and father, but when away from home he oftentimes lived recklessly.

Tom had beautiful blue eyes. His black hair was always in disarray when he removed the hard hat he was compelled to wear in the steel mills where he sold his company's wares for the steel-making process. His perfect facial features made up for his lack of height, and his muscular build invited women to be enveloped into his arms. His smile that showed his perfect white teeth and his voice when he said "Let's go to bed" convinced his many slaves to obey his sexual, make-love desires.

He lifted weights to enhance his build. He consumed twelve vitamin pills daily. When the waitresses asked, "Why all the pills?" when they saw them spread out on the table before him, his response was, "I'm dying, and I want to make love to you before I go. Say when."

He sauntered with his feet pointed outward when

he walked due to years of having to tread through harsh gravel in the mills. If he had a hard-on, he couldn't walk.

One day he became enraptured with a new desk clerk at the motel and could not move for half an hour, leaning on the counter of sundries for sale while looking at her. He was a sucker for a pretty face and fell in love with all who said yes to him.

Tom was a married man with a lovely wife whom he adored and three children whom he loved. He was a traveling salesman. He was having fun away from home.

It was the year 1962. The disease AIDS was not prevalent then. Some salesmen had to pay for sexual pleasure. Some salesmen, usually the handsome ones, got it free. Some salesmen went home to their wives.

Some waitresses slept around; some did not. However, flirting brought larger tips; their uniform pockets bulged with change and bills.

Shelly and Norma Jean were both waitresses working the breakfast and lunch shifts in the motel restaurant. They with their respective families migrated from the South to the Midwest. Both husbands were coast-to-coast truck drivers and were gone for long periods of time. Both wives knew their husbands slept around, so they did the same, had fun doing it, compared notes often, and were not astonished to know of Tom Stevens's indiscretions.

Shelly, in her early thirties and five-foot-two in stature, was the cutest, bubbliest young woman with big blue eyes, black hair, and an eversmile—she sparkled. The black and white aproned uniform she wore did not deter from her sexuality. Her hips were rather large and her boobs didn't show much promise of being a handful to a man, but the customers loved her and asked for her to be their waitress. Many wanted to bed her. She said yes to the best tippers and yes to the very handsome, irresistible Tom Stevens.

She went home laughing every workday. It was most fun to get home and have her two young girls watch while she counted her tip money, added it to her record totals, and then dumped it all into a gunnysack that only her husband could lift and take to the bank periodically. She saved for her trips back home to south Georgia to see her family at least twice a year.

Norma Jean was just the opposite of her waitress friend Shelly. She did not sparkle. She was quiet, almost shy, with a soft-spoken voice. Her hair was red, her face square. She was average looking, but oh, her walk! She moved like a slithering snake. If a customer was hurrying to eat his eggs for breakfast, they got cold—the eggs could wait, but not the sight of Norma Jean as she walked, pouring coffee, taking orders, serving the orders. They watched, saying to themselves, "God, I'll bet she's great in bed."

When she was asked to have some fun, she never said yes—she answered "S . . . u . . . r . . . e" just as slowly as her slithering walk. Arrangements would be made, knowing she would quietly perform and sock away her love-making money just in case her truck driver husband should leave her for another woman in his travels and never come back.

She was a calculated sleep-around waitress in her late thirties who felt no one knew she was being unfaithful to her moral obligations just for the money.

Norma Jean was not talkative, granting her a very private life. Her married daughter never suspected her insipid mother could live so dangerously.

Mary and Ruth were the other two breakfast and lunch waitresses. They were in their forties with graying hair on Mary and dyed red hair on Ruth. They each had families. Fucking around did not interest them at all. They went home with less tips, but it was good enough. Their husbands were the breadwinners. They worked for extra money for the children and the house. Screw the gals who spread their legs to strangers from all over the world. It was a sin.

Mary and Ruth were Catholic. They overlooked the obvious violation of God's law by their coworkers, who were likeable and fun to be around. To each his own. Who were they to judge? This was the working world. Who cared?

The south side of Chicago housed U.S. Steel Corporation, Interlake, Youngstown, Republic, and Inland Steel mills. Numerous industries using their by-products filled the surrounding area like a spider's web. This brought in many salesmen to frequent the area, reserving rooms for sleeping usually by the week in the three large motels in the area—two Holiday Inns and the Southtown Motel. The steadies, as they were called, were the most welcome, respected guests. Repeat customers paid the bills, management perceived.

The Southtown Motel consisted of one hundred and ten rooms on two floors of a red brick building shaped like a T. Three rooms were two-room suites, and all rooms were furnished with two double beds for sleeping accommodations—of course every room had a shower, wash basin, and commode. A restaurant and bar facility was just off the entrance, and a large outdoor swimming pool in the rear of the premises was visible through the dining room windows. The front desk and small office were to the right of the entry. Seating arrangements with tables, two small red couches, four matching chairs, tall ferns, and tall lamps adorned an area where guests waited for a ride to wherever or just came out of their rooms for a change of scenery or to read the newspaper. Red and black Scotch plaid printed carpeting covered the floors throughout and looked quite worn in many areas; housekeeping hesitated to vacuum every day for fear of adding to the very threadbare walking areas. Rather dingy, beige, rough-textured draperies covered windows in the lobby from ceiling to floor. Housekeeping opened these drapes during the day and used to close them come evening; however, now they stayed open day and night so as not to expose the sun-faded areas.

Some lamps in the rooms and even in the hallways were in need of lightbulbs, but maintenance had no spares. Bedspreads in the rooms needed replacement, but no funds were available to do so. The whole place looked shabby.

When darkness fell, upon entry, the place looked and sounded romantic and fun, with music coming from the piano bar accompanied by sing-along customers. Dim lights hid all the flaws of the aging decor.

Chapter Two

The Hired Help

Nina was an experienced switchboard operator who applied for part-time work at the motel with aspirations of having extra Christmas spending money. No openings were available at the time she applied, but the manager liked her immediately—her smile, long blonde hair, and slim figure at the age of twenty-eight. A sweet voice and skilled background according to the application told him to hire her at the first opening. Three years as telephone operator with Illinois Bell qualified her for the job. Two weeks later he called her to come to work part time. She began working full time when her only son, Rickey, began school in the first grade. She stayed eight years.

The manager was the desk clerk as well. His wife was the housekeeper. The maintenance man smelled of liquor throughout his work day, even in the early morning. There were problems during the course of the workday that took Greg Powers, the manager, away from the desk, so he soon added more responsibilities onto Nina.

You see, Greg was really not the manager; he was the desk clerk who appointed himself manager for propriety. Should someone ask to talk to the manager, there should be one—there was none. Greg looked like a manager should look—rather handsome, in his middle fifties with a slim mustache and silver-streaked hair; best of all, he always wore a bow tie, white shirt, and black suit. He greeted men and women with a "Yes sir" and "Yes ma'am" and seemed to want to bow before them and click his heels.

He calculated and sent to the home office the daily reports of occupancy. This chore he soon turned over to Nina, leaving him free to do other tasks, of which there were many: the ice machine broke down, maintenance can't fix it, there will be no ice for the bar and no ice water for the restaurant come lunchtime; the cook is threatening to quit because the kitchen exhaust fan went out; both houseboys did not show up for work so Greg had to do their job because the maids found a chore much too heavy a task; and worst of all, too many television sets are out of order and there are none to replace them with until they can find a service to come to the motel.

When outside contractors had to be called in for necessary repairs, the invoices were sent to the home office in Cleveland, Ohio for payment. The home office did not pay their bills for six months. This tardiness made it difficult to obtain service when needed.

Greg soon taught desk duties to Nina as well. She caught on quickly, giving Greg more time to do what he could to maintain order.

Greg's wife Dorothy, a fiftyish woman having a pretty, round face and somewhat round body, managed housekeeping to the best of her ability and availability of supplies and kept cleanliness throughout with her staff of houseboys who came and went. They were young boys working for the summer or high school dropouts who stayed until they could get a better paying job. The maids were all there as long as she had been there, and that was five years.

No bosses with explicit orders to do this or that—or else—were ever on the premises. No stress existed. However, everyone did his or her job to please the guests who were paying customers; they owed this in return for their paycheck.

The restaurant was leased to Harry and Louie Katz—brothers, both in their sixties, both having a scant amount of gray hair, slight in build and with glasses. They also leased the bar that was tended to during the day by the very Italian-looking Art and by sleek-haired, Greek-looking Damien during the evening hours. Bar hours were 11:00 A.M. to 4:00 A.M. Harry policed their investment during the day, and Louie at night. They seldom sat down. They did not trust the hired help. They did not even eat there because they did not want to eat the profits; they carried a brown paper bag from home. Can you imagine—they had a restaurant with foods galore and they brown-bagged—Kosher brown-bagged? Gads! Ya gotta just shake your head and wonder why—poor ol' guys.

Harry and Louie walked holding their hands behind them, heads slightly downward but eyes ever open wide, looking for the thieves they suspected were lessening their bank deposit profits for their retirement to Florida one day.

Georgia Greenly, a tall, thin brunette who wore glasses that did not fit—they were forever falling down on her nose—handled the receipts from restaurant and bar. She had an office in one room on the first floor set aside for this function as part of the lease agreement for the Jewish brothers. She did not dare be dishonest in her work, knowing her bosses would do whatever needed to be done to retrieve their losses. Although the opportunity was there, it was not worth it.

Georgia was close to having ulcers and had migraine headaches frequently due to stress. The Katz brothers were not easy men to work for. Their first love was money.

No laughter existed in their management, not even smiles nor thank-yous nor blessings for a job well done. They showed reluctance to give the large tips awarded to the waitresses who served food on large trays to the upstairs meeting rooms when rented and even asked them for a share. The girls were so used to their greed that they did not object, saying, "Okay, if you carry the heavy trays up the stairs for us." This shut them up.

The Southtown Motel was part of a chain; however, each unit had its own name throughout the Midwest. Some units were very profitable and well maintained, but some were not.

This one was not a moneymaker; it was a tax write-off against the profits of the other twelve motels owned by the owners in Cleveland, Ohio, that was soon to expire for this tax purpose. They were bleeding this one dry.

No monies were being spent for repairs, replacement of worn furnishings, or the expense of a manager on duty at all times. One of the owners came in once every three months to check on things and after each visit said, "All is well. Carry on."

Now, there had been no one to check for the past six months—no one cared, it was assumed. Employees worked for payday. No one gave a damn except to please the guests. They all did their jobs. They all waited to see what was going to happen. Something had to happen to this phantom motel soon or it would fall apart. Occupancy was averaging sixty percent, while the other equivalent motels in the area were doing eighty-five percent. Something was wrong. Something had been wrong for a long time. Everyone knew the motel could not go on like this and survive.

Chapter Three

Aldo

It wasn't long before Aldo Marchezzi walked into the motel and announced he was sent from the home office to be the manager of the Southtown Motel.

Aldo was not too tall, very slim (I mean *slim*), graying at the temples, had an Italian accent in speech, and smoked perpetually. The semismile on his clean-shaven face gave some the impression that he was jovial, but another impression was that he was sinister and could not be trusted.

He came in. He took over. He allowed everyone to do his or her job without question.

He did not live there. He came and he went as if there was nothing to do or question or supervise.

Everyone liked him. He had no negatives to say about the place or any who worked there.

He didn't even dress like a manager. He never wore a suit or tie, just pants and a shirt with a pocket to hold his cigarette habit; his lighter he carried in his pants pocket. His shoes were slip-on loafers. He walked with his hands in his pockets most of the time, hiding his yellow-stained smoking fingers.

It was soon learned that he took residence in a

condo across the street from the motel with his girlfriend, Diane, a divorcée with two grown children.
She was blonde, blue eyed, and gorgeous. Diane
played the horses and the numbers. She gambled
heavily, her bad, costly habit.

Aldo tried to get her to stop or just to slow down,
but she was hooked, thinking she would one day win
big, as all gamblers wish.

Diane was just as thin as Aldo. She also smoked.
Altogether they made a handsome couple. She too
wore loafers covering her feet due to having ingrown
toenails caused by wearing high-heeled shoes for
many years in her quest to look glamorous in her
youth.

Still, nothing was being done to refurbish the
amenities of the motel. Occupancy remained the same.
The only changes that occurred were that the high-
priced desk clerk, Greg, serving as the self-appointed
manager, was let go, as was his wife Dorothy, the
housekeeper.

One of the maids was appointed housekeeper at a
lesser salary. The desk clerk and the switchboard operator handled reservations and check-ins and checkouts. Albert, the alcoholic maintenance man, remained
on the job. His knowledge of running and maintain-
ing motel machinery was sorely needed to be related
to another maintenance man before considering his
release from the job he had held for ten years—ever
since the motel opened.

The next thing that happened was that the restaurant and bar lease expired, and Harry and Louie Katz
were gone. They did not even say good-bye to the
employees who had worked for them for many years.

They didn't care—they were on their way to Florida's sunshine, never again to carry a brown bag to work.

The restaurant and bar were now under the supervision of the motel. This was the reason for the newly appointed manager, a huge responsibility requiring an experienced person—Aldo Marchezzi.

Aldo's girlfriend Diane came often for complimentary breakfast, lunch, and dinner, always with a cigarette in her hand, shuffling along in her slippers and nevertheless looking sexy as hell.

Soon, suites and rooms were being logged by the desk clerk on order of Aldo as complimentary. He announced, "These are my friends, and I can have my friends stay here free of charge."

No one disputed the new Italian manager with the sinister yet friendly grin.

Employees thought he was great. How dare anyone question what he did for his friends? Only a first male name was on the room registration; no one ever came to the desk to sign in. Aldo simply announced, "Put that room under so-and-so's name—complimentary." It was his right as manager.

One morning after a few months went by, at around 11:00 A.M., two significant looking men wearing business suits, white shirts, and ties, looking like they were in their late forties, entered the motel lobby and approached the desk while Nina was on duty. They both produced FBI credentials, and one of the men displayed a photo of a man, asking if he was ever seen on the premises.

"Sure," Nina answered without hesitation, having immediately recognized a guest in the photo. "He's been living here for months. He's in the dining room right now."

"Show us," one of the men said as he put away the photo and both men placed their identifications into their suit pockets.

Nina added, "I'll go get a cup of coffee and look to see where he is. I'll come back and tell you."

She did not realize the gravity of the situation, having no past experiences in connection with the law; she was just simply leading to the identification of someone the two men were looking for . . . no big deal.

She went for the coffee and saw that the man in the photo was seated in the corner at the two-top reserved for waitresses and/or hostesses. As she poured coffee into a cup, she turned to see the two FBI men walk into the dining room, not waiting for her to go back to the desk. Immediately catching sight of their man, they went right up to him, said his name, produced their badges, and said "Come with us."

They left the dining room without incident, having handcuffed their man, each taking him by the arm and escorting him to his room, amazingly as easy as that—what luck!

The employees were very surprised to see this man taken away; he was liked by everyone. He was quiet, he bothered no one, and best of all, he was a good tipper to the waitresses and maids. It was later learned via the newspaper that he was the number one most wanted criminal by the FBI and the leader of a gang who tortured people during robberies in wealthy sections of big cities, the latest being the north side of Chicago on the Gold Coast—the elite side. The fugitive from the law had been hiding out in the Southtown Motel for many months in a complimentary room.

After the FBI captured its number one most wanted man, Nina became suspicious of Aldo. As much as she liked him, she knew all was not right—too many comp rooms—no faces of occupants—too many comp restaurant charges. And why did the boss come and go so much?

Yet he always asked everyone, "How are you?" making his words sound like he really cared about people. He showed respect for all the employees, and they in return reciprocated, feeling he must have a big, kind heart.

Chapter Four

The Rat

One day some months later, one of the motel owners from Cleveland, Ohio, and his wife surprised the employees with a visit. Usually one of the owners—there were three in the same family, two brothers and a son of one of them—telephoned first to say when they intended to arrive, but not this time. Of course the man and his wife were given one of the three suites on the second floor of the motel. They notified the desk clerk they would be staying two days, thinking the suite they were occupying might be needed to fill a reservation—the front desk should know.

Aldo was most courteous as host. The lobby and hallways were hurriedly cleaned as never before. Everyone was on best behavior. All was well. The restaurant, bar, and motel were doing as good as could be. Reports to the home office were always timely.

The owner was satisfied. The main purpose of their visit was for the man to take his wife on a shopping spree in downtown Chicago. This was just a stopover, not a check of the premises and their investment, as expected by all who worked there and wondered if the owners finally knew of misgivings in their motel.

Now, Karen was the night hostess in the dining room. She looked like Sophia Loren, very Greek, with full, glossed lips, five-foot-four, dark hair, brown eyes, meticulous in her attire, always wearing outstanding jewelry with each outfit. Her hobby was shopping, and of course buying. These excursions made her late for work often.

Karen knew the frequency of restaurant charges that were being comped and felt this was not right— it was dishonest. She felt this was the time to do something. Someone had to report to the owners all the suspected wrongdoing. This was her chance—the owners were here and perhaps they cared to know.

Karen did not get home until way past midnight— too late to be calling their motel room—and was reluctant to call while on duty in the dining room for fear of being overheard. She suggested that Nina call their suite that evening when she was in the privacy of her home.

So Nina telephoned their room around 10:00 P.M. and asked the owner to send a spy to check on things, stating she did not know if there were wrongdoings, just too many comp rooms and restaurant charges. The owner said he would take it from there and thanked her for the information.

The next morning it was 7:00 A.M. when Charles, the nice looking young night auditor, called Nina at home to warn her that Steve, the six-foot college student working part time as evening desk clerk, was on duty when she had called the motel owner's suite. He recognized her voice and listened in on her phone call. Steve told Aldo that Nina had reported to the owner that there were many comp rooms and restaurant charges and suggested that the owner look into the accusations and find out if true or false or insignificant to proper motel management.

Karen and Nina both had thoughts of dishonesty. Steve told Aldo and then told Charles, who told Nina, and now Nina feared for her life.

To snitch on a man who looked like he represents Mafioso is to make one's hands shake and heart thump faster and be uncertain as to what the next move should be.

To stay home and not report for the day shift was to admit guilt.

Nina chose to go to work and take her medicine, trusting that truth wins over all. After all, she didn't report Aldo doing anything criminal, just that someone should check on things; Karen was the one who was truly concerned.

She went to work as though nothing had happened, saying good morning to everyone. Aldo was waiting for her. He went into the dining room for a cup of coffee. This gave Nina a chance to settle in, count the cash drawer, take a deep breath, and hope for the best.

Aldo came to the desk and immediately said, "I know what you did. Why did you do that? I am manager of this motel and I am entitled to have complimentary rooms for my friends. You are a good girl. I like you. You do good work. Let us forget about this. The owner is leaving today and agrees with me that I can comp rooms for my friends. There is no problem. Okay?"

Aldo told her this with that half-smile, half-sneer that only he could execute. And he was dressed in a

suit, shirt, and tie for the first time—much to everyone's surprise.

Nina's heartbeats slowed down as she answered,
"Okay" and said she was sorry for the misunderstand-
ing. She also told him it would never happen again.
She never mentioned Karen's name. Aldo was not
aware that Karen also suspected wrongdoing in the
motel.

Nina went about her duties as desk clerk; however,
Aldo never left the desk area all that day. He smoked a
pack of Camel cigarettes, even had coffee brought to
him rather than leave for a minute, until the owner and
his wife checked out around 4:00 P.M., just before time
for Nina's shift to end.

Aldo hadn't eaten anything all that day; no wonder
he was so thin. Nina gathered that he was one nervous
son of a bitch—there had to be something wrong.

Everything went back to normal. The freebee
rooms and food increased. No one saw the unregis-
tered guests who occupied these rooms except the
maids. They knew nothing of any discrepancies; it was
just another room to clean, another unknown guest.
They came and they went, and the maids were ever
grateful for the tips they left.

Nina was glad that Aldo liked her. Little by little she
relaxed the fear of her car being blown up, of being
shot to death en route to work, or of being beaten to
death in her own garage before entering her home.

She liked Aldo and decided to mind her own business, do her job for the money, and let Karen bitch
about her own gripes. She was tired of the stress all this
had brought upon her; it was not worth it.

Chapter Five

The Major

Two months later a retired army major by the name of John Cavanaugh and his wife Susan came to spy on the workings of the Southtown Motel on the pretext that the owners were contemplating the sale of the motel and needed a firsthand report as to conditions of the restaurant, lounge, rooms, and premises.

Now, Georgia was a nervous wreck. She handled all the restaurant and bar revenues even after Harry and Louie Katz left. She continued to occupy the same office on the first floor of the motel. She also made motel revenue deposits for the Brink's pickup. Well, now she was guilty of having given Aldo thousands of dollars on loan to his girlfriend Diane, with no sign of him ever returning the funds into the restaurant account. Motel receipts had to balance with the reports of occupancy to the home office, lessening chances for discrepancies—restaurant and bar figures were being played with.

Georgia began drinking heavily. Hard liquor created a strong odor on her breath at 8 A.M. when she reported for work. Nina was concerned for her, knowing her husband was out of work at the time and she had two children with many needs. Everyone was aware of her strong liquid habit that was sure to lose her her job.

One morning Nina asked Georgia what was wrong when she could see that Georgia could not walk straight after clearing all the lounge tape receipts from the register before beginning her work with the daily deposit.

Georgia's hands were shaking, her lips were trembling, and she reeked of booze as she whispered and answered Nina's question, "I gave Aldo seven thousand dollars of restaurant money to give to his girlfriend Diane, who was supposed to return it long ago. I'm afraid that in an audit it will be discovered and I'll lose my job. I don't know what to do." She was close to tears and needed another drink.

She was a weak woman who was a victim of circumstances subjected by her boss, his girlfriend, their weaknesses, and deceit.

Nina's response was to tell her to make sure the money was replaced or else she would go to jail. She watched Georgia's staggering walk en route to her office, wondering if she was going to fall and pass out.

Five days later, with once again trembling hands and lips when filling her morning coffee cup, Georgia whispered to Nina, not to be overheard, that the money was replaced and deposited.

Whew! Thank God! At an opportune time, Nina whispered the news to John Cavanaugh while at the coffee machine. He was pleased, nodding his head and actually smiling, just saying one word. She did not want Aldo to see her talking to the spy sent from the home office, so she didn't even look up to see his smile or his nod. She did, however, hear him say, "Good."

A short time later Georgia was fired. She had expected it, realizing she had no one to blame but herself for being guilty as an accomplice and an alcoholic obeying her Italian motel manager, thinking, "What else could I have done; he was my boss." Her tears impaired her speech, so she just waved a good-bye when going out the door carrying a box with belongings.

Aldo was told new owners were coming in and his services would no longer be needed.

When everything settled back to normal, Nina asked John Cavanaugh why Aldo was not being charged with illegalities. He told her the FBI was working on deporting him back to Italy for harboring Mafia fugitives in the motels he had been managing over the years throughout the Midwest. They were looking for bigger offenses than complimentary rooms and food to charge him with. They needed proof of association with the underworld, and it was hard to come by.

Everybody had to play it cool. It was out of their hands.

Too bad. Aldo was liked by all, but all were glad to be rid of the tension and stress of knowing something was not right for so long a time.

Major John Cavanaugh had been a career soldier. He walked like one. He looked like one. He was six-foot-two, square shouldered, gray haired, impressive looking, and soft spoken. He seemed relaxed, but in one abrupt movement his voice could get anyone's attention. He gave commands for many years. In return he expected a "Yes, sir!"

However, his new job upon retirement was in a different world, the world of civilians, who were not accustomed to taking orders, especially after not having had a real manager for years and then a boss who let things be while he came and went as he pleased, having no one to answer to while he took care of his friends on the premises free of charge.

The motel employees included houseboys who were sloppy in their work. Bundles of soiled linens and towels were dragged on the floor hallways, often left for long periods of time while the houseboys conversed with the maids or stopped to rest. This clutter looked untidy to the guests who could hardly pass through the hallways—especially when carrying luggage. These bundles should have been placed on carts or over their shoulders for quick deposit in their proper place in the housekeeping department to be picked up by the laundry service each day.

The maids congregated to gossip on coffee breaks, at lunchtime, and once again during an afternoon coffee break, taking longer than the fifteen minutes allowed.

The maintenance man always stopped at the front desk to converse rather than hasten to his work mechanics.

The desk clerk made personal phone calls.

The switchboard operator polished her nails on the job, and three rings rang before the incoming calls were answered.

The night hostess was never on time. It was a quiet

time from 5:00 P.M. to 6:00 P.M. when dinner started, so what was the rush?

The daytime hostess expected the morning waitresses, who were always on time, to open up and tend to the cash register as well. What was the hurry? It was early morning; the place wouldn't fall apart.

The busboys ate too much food in the kitchen. They were teenagers and were always hungry.

The waitresses spent too much time talking to guests.

The hostess did not jump when a guest came to the register to pay the bill.

Major John Cavanaugh would have fired every goddamned employee in the fucking motel. If they were in the army he would have seen to it that they were all sentenced to hard labor for insubordination. This was his summation of the new responsibilities that made his blood boil. If he had the power, everyone would serve two years in the army right after high school to be taught discipline, neatness, and most of all, respect for following orders—men as well as women.

These perceptions he told his wife almost daily. She agreed with him, having lived the army way most of her sixtyish years.

So Major John Cavanaugh resolved that he would stay in his office, the room designated on the first floor that Georgia had occupied. Susan, his lovely, white-haired wife, who had a very pleasant southern accent and matching disposition, was now doing the bookkeeping financial work. The help were left alone to run the motel as they were accustomed. The major and his wife knew they would be there for a short time. Aldo was leaving. The home office discharged him. He didn't even say good-bye.

They did their spy work. Aldo and Georgia were gone. The freebee rooms were now unoccupied. To correct all imperfections to perfection would most probably give him a heart attack, his wife advised. So, why fight it? Let it all be. Who cares?

He checked on things in the morning when he and his wife had breakfast, then at lunchtime he walked around and checked again. He was accustomed when in the army for all underlings to come to him. So, come 4:00 P.M., he did not leave the office—Nina went to him. She made notes of all the day's happenings, reported expected occupancy numbers for that evening, and related all issues to her superior, soldier boss. He nodded his head in approval, seldom asking a question or commenting on her decisions. She would say, "That's all, sir. Good night, sir," and take her leave, always feeling she should be saluting him.

He thought, "Goddamn, what a fine soldier she would have made. She deserves lieutenant bars." He even nodded his head in approval without saying a word when she told him Albert, the maintenance man, was so drunk one day that he could hardly walk or talk. Rather than tell the major, she chose to handle it as she did everything else, without bothering him. She had one of the houseboys take him home to sleep it off so as not to risk Albert losing his job, knowing if the major had seen him in this condition and there had been a brig on the premises, he would have thrown him in it and thrown the keys away—the drunken son of a bitch.

What John Cavanaugh did not know was that

Albert and his wife argued daily about his drinking problem, and she was now threatening to leave him. This fact made him drink even more. He was a gentle, loving, kind man who needed compassion and understanding from those around him, especially his wife and son, but all they did was scream at him, call him a stupid Polack, and then tell him to die and go to hell.

Nina knew he needed help; he was a nice man, and he knew motel mechanics. The major was tough and coldhearted and didn't give a shit about anything but the army way, but he stayed in his office and let Nina take care of everything, to the many thanks of the employees.

A few months later the Cavanaugh's had a going away party announcing the end of their tenure/spy work at the motel and that the new owners would soon be arriving to take over command.

They said their good-byes and wondered where their next assignment would take them in the employ of motels in need of surveillance.

Chapter Six

Guy and Joe

A few months later two young men introduced themselves to the employees as the new owners of the Southtown Motel. Guy and Joe Campbell were brothers. They did not look like brothers. Guy was older, in his late thirties, and much shorter than Joe, who was in his early thirties. They did not purchase the property; it would have taken millions. They leased it from the chain, who could no longer use it as a tax write-off.

The hired help was muttering, "Holy cow! New bosses again," except that most of them said, "Holy shit! New bosses again."

They settled in. They purchased houses in the immediate area, knowing they would be spending a great deal of time at a motel that was active day and night, seven days a week and all holidays.

Guy handled all the money and paperwork. Joe ran around checking on the desk, housekeeping, restaurant, and lounge. They were fair in settling all problems, they were well liked, all was calm, and everyone was doing his or her job—they finally had owners on the premises who cared.

They even kept the alcoholic maintenance man on his job, with Joe keeping a sharp eye on him in order to learn all the mechanics of the place: the huge boil-er in the basement for heat, the air-conditioning unit, everything electrical, hot water heater, ice machines, and kitchen equipment. Due to the fact that Joe had no previous knowledge of liquor for the bar or food for the restaurant, these departments needed his full-time attention as well.

The best part is that Albert had not had a drink while on the job since they came to govern.

When they perceived how well and how quickly Nina made up the reports on occupancy, handled the switchboard, took reservations, and even worked the desk check-ins and checkouts, they gave her the title of manager. For their lease agreement they were informed by their attorney that they needed to name a president, vice president, and manager. Of course Guy was president, Joe was vice president.

Nina felt awkward for a while, since she had only worked there seven months and now had a title and cards printed for the occasion that adorned the front desk, but everyone felt she was the best suited for the job.

She was their manager for the next seven and a half years.

It wasn't long before Nina was called into the office and asked to perform yet another function. The new owners learned by reviewing all registrations, looking for company names in connection with guests, that most of the large surrounding corporations were not represented. She was asked to be ambassador of the Southtown Motel, in hopes of finding out why these corporations did not send their traveling personnel to the Southtown, which was the closest in location to their plants than any other motel in the area.

When Guy mentioned Ford Motor Company as first on the list, Nina was alerted and responded with, "I worked there for two years until my job was cut out of the budget when I was in the Cost Analysis Department. I know my way around that plant, and the traffic manager is someone who attended the same school I did."

So, on the road she went, somewhat nervous, yet knowing she had a job to do for the now very nice new owners of the motel she was manager of.

She was ushered into the office of Jack McGinnis, whom she immediately recognized as having been two years ahead of her in classes. He had had a steady girlfriend then. They were often seen kissing at her locker in school. Everyone knew they would be married some day. It was that obvious, and they did marry upon graduation as reported in the hometown newspaper.

He was just as handsome now as in school. He now had a top job at Ford Motor Company, moving equipment as well as personnel to and from the plant as traffic manger.

Nina told him the purpose of her visit, saying, "I represent the Southtown Motel as manager. We know we do not get any of your reservations or meeting room business at our facility. Do you know why?"

She folded her hands in her lap and waited for him to reply. Nina had dressed the part of a business woman, wearing her best black suit, a white blouse, high-heeled shoes, and carrying a black bag that held cards stating she was manager along with a colorful brochure of the motel she was representing.

Jack stopped his movements behind his desk. He had been shuffling papers, answering telephone calls, signing his name to paperwork, and answering questions for employees with a seemingly endless stream of problems needing answers. He was in charge in this department, a massive room of desks, personnel, and telephones.

Nina had time to look around the room until he could give her his undivided attention. What she noticed was that all men in the department wore their shirt sleeves rolled up, and the phones on all the desks had headsets, leaving hands free for paperwork.

"Do you really want to know this? I mean, are you ready for the truth?" Jack asked as he looked directly into Nina's eyes and wondered if he should or shouldn't tell her the harsh truth.

"That's why I'm here. Come on, tell me. The new owners want to know," she answered, determined to do her job and make her employers proud of her. She steadily looked into his unwavering eyes.

"Okay," he said as he put down his pen, rolled back away from his desk, and began: "We used to use your rooms for personnel from all our Ford plants who came to our assembly plant because your motel is so close by. We especially used your meeting rooms and restaurant services for our conferences because we have no space here for that purpose. Your restaurant managers brought in whores to sexually engage our men. A wife of one of our men from Detroit's home office learned of this somehow and contacted the home office. As a result a bulletin was issued to all personnel stating that if any charges from the Southtown Motel in Chicago, Illinois, appeared on their expense reports, reimbursement would not be made by Ford Motor."

Nina listened, then thanked him for his explanation

and his time and most of all for being so candid with information that was hidden for so many years. She said she would go back and advise the new owners, proud of herself that she kept her mouth from dropping open to show her shock and dismay at his reply to her question.

By the time she drove back to the motel she was trembling and in tears. Guy Campbell ushered her into his office, closed the door, and listened to her relate her story: "I quit. I am ashamed to work here. I can't represent this place. I just learned from someone I went to school with that call girls (she could not say the word *whores*) were brought in by our restaurant managers to the Ford meetings here."

She recounted the rest of the details, blew her nose, and wiped her tears before sipping on the coffee Guy had a waitress bring to the door. She was still shaken, but began to relax somewhat.

"I am so proud of you, Nina," Guy admitted with a small grin while nodding his head. "You have accomplished something no one else could have done. You learned exactly what we wanted to know. You did a great job. Don't worry, we will do what we must do to make things right."

He grasped her shoulder tightly with admiration and told her she need not go on the road any more that day; the shock was too much for her tender years.

She fixed her red eyes in the washroom and spent the rest of the day at the desk in front where she was most comfortable, smiling at everyone. She was grateful that the switchboard operator did not question her.

Before the end of the day, Guy and Joe asked her to go to Allis Chalmers, another close-by plant whose room business had ceased years before, including meeting rooms and food service.

After taking a deep breath and releasing a big sigh, she did not object to their request, thinking she must trust these new owners to vindicate the bad reputation of the place where she loved working. She was just doing her job as asked.

Well, wouldn't you know she learned the same reason from Allis Chalmers as was told to her by Ford Motor, only this time it was a woman who answered her questions.

It was common knowledge that prostitutes frequented the lounge at all hours. This large company could not excuse this practice.

Nina asked the personnel manger she was talking to if everything was cleaned up, would their personnel patronize the motel, restaurant, and meeting rooms? The lady answered that they might consider it due to the close proximity to their establishment and the fact that they had no meeting rooms on their premises and no restaurant as close by as the Southtown Motel.

Hearing these reasons for a second time made it easier for Nina to digest. Perhaps because she was talking to a woman, she was not as ashamed. She did not shed tears this time. She went back to the motel laughing and swearing and exclaiming, "Son of a bitch, this place is just a whorehouse!" She was still laughing when she told Guy what she had learned, and he laughed with her. Once again Guy was proud of his newly appointed manager. He couldn't have chosen a better one—she was a gem.

Nina continued her travels all that week to all surrounding companies, handed them her calling card and brochure, announced the new owners, and asked for their reservations for their out-of-town personnel. The brochure explained the availability of rooms, the restaurant, and meeting rooms. Her visits were quick, stating appreciation, thank you, and please use our facility.

Nina's salary was increased for her very disconcerting revelations and so were her duties. It was usually quiet during the day on the desk after checkouts, so Guy taught her payroll, gave her her own desk in the back room just off the front desk area, and later added the checkbook, giving her signature privilege on checks so she could pay the bills, make deposits for the Brink's pickup, and handle petty cash.

Common sense and her honesty enabled her to whisk through her many duties and still have control of the front desk and all its responsibilities, especially having the right amount of rooms to fill all reservations that were being taken. To overbook on reservations could cause the loss of a steady guest should they arrive late at night, having guaranteed a room with a credit card, and find none available. The loss of a steady is another motel's gain—two Holiday Inns were just minutes away.

Guy and Joe composed a letter that was sent to all companies whose business they anticipated, advising them of the fact that Harry and Louie Katz no longer owned the restaurant, meeting rooms, or lounge at the Southtown Motel. They were the new owners.

They also stated they were aware of certain indiscretions that existed under the former ownership but that this management did not condone any such practices. Their patronage would be greatly appreciated.

Hurray! It worked. All companies became customers

again after about a five-year absence. Meeting room business flourished. Good cooks were hired for the kitchen. Breakfast and lunch were always packed—even the evening steaks with huge mushrooms were best sellers. Money was available to refurbish window dressings, new carpeting was installed throughout, and even new bedspreads adorned the rooms. Best of all, television sets that were too costly to repair were replaced by new units in all rooms, much to the joy of Albert, who always had to attempt to please guests when they would report out-of-order sets by switching sets from room to room in search of a working set, a most heavy task.

All was functioning to the best of occupancy in years, enabling Guy Campbell to go on to Oregon to lease a Holiday Inn motel. He left Joe in charge, knowing Nina would watch over all—especially over Joe.

As young as she was, Nina became the matriarch. All employees respected her steadfast honesty, caring, ability to solve problems, and understanding of human relations when they needed days off, sick leave, or consolation.

Joe was scoffed at behind his back due to his incompetence, quick decisions (usually the wrong ones), and showing he could not care less about the motel.

He found a new love—he bought an airplane, a two-seater Piper Cub. He asked anyone and everyone to go flying with him. A muscular houseboy named Mike and a new, young, attractive, tall, brunette, single, part-time morning waitress who finished her shift at 2:00 P.M. often accompanied him on his flights.

Chapter Seven

Alice

Now, Joe had a beautiful young wife named Alice and two young children, both girls. Alice had sky blue eyes, long blonde hair, an exquisite complexion, and nice clothes, but—here comes the kicker—her constant gum chewing/cracking habit was a sure sign of no class or some hidden anger. It spoiled her beauty. She came to the motel often with her three- and four-year-old daughters, who were just as blonde and pretty as their mother.

"What are you doing here?" was Alice's greeting from Joe each time she entered the dining room in hopes of seeing her husband and children's father. Joe expressly wanted his wife to stay home and care for the children so that he could have a separate life from his motel work.

Alice was afraid to fly and would never go up. She was a mother. Her girls needed her. Heaven forbid if something bad happened to their mother.

But she continued to show up at the motel, aggravate Joe, and look over the situation to fulfill her obsession with jealousy.

Many times Joe was already flying when she got

there, and she realized that if Nina was not so good at her job, her husband wouldn't be free to fly so much.

Alice had no freedom. She was envious of her sister-in-law, Guy's wife Joan, who had six children, a housekeeper, and babysitters and came to the motel frequently to see her husband. Joan was greeted warmly by Guy and invited for coffee and/or food in the dining room. She even took the time to stop at the front desk and talk to the hired help, pleasing her husband, who thought employees needed to be treated with respect; after all, the profits of the motel depended on the services administered by the hired help.

Alice was not permitted to have babysitters nor a housekeeper—Joe did not allow it. He loved his children immensely and insisted that his wife care for them. Her two girls were always with her when she went to the motel. She never stopped to talk to any of the help; she just chewed her gum and said hello or just nodded her head, saying, "Hi." Joe had her leave as soon as possible, not even offering her a cup of coffee, even though they sat at a table in the dining room.

He did not want her anywhere but at home. When she had to go to the beauty shop for her blonde treatment, he stayed home with the girls until she returned.

Alice was jealous of Nina, her husband's right arm. Joe bragged about her all the time. Nina was too pretty, too smart, too everything. Alice was also jealous of all the waitresses who were pretty or sexy and went home wondering which one her husband was screwing.

But things were going well. All was in control. A great staff. Joe bought a larger plane and began flying even in early mornings, especially when knowing rain was predicted come afternoon.

One morning when Nina arrived on the job at 8:00 A.M., the night clerk whom she relieved told the mother manager that he suspected a prostitute in Room 136, just past the lounge on the first floor. Many men came to ask for her room throughout the night—solicitation was quite obvious.

Nina said she would look into it and thanked him for reporting it to her. Both agreed something had to be done.

By 10:00 A.M. there were five calls from men to her room asking for an appointment time to visit. Nina listened in on her phone calls as she had learned to do, by removing the headset jack from the switchboard, inserting it again ever so slightly, pressing it down, then opening the switchboard key without even so much as a click on the line to be heard by the other party. She could hear everything.

This was not enough proof to call the police, just suspicions. Then one by one the night waitresses, bellhops, busboys, and the night hostess called Nina on the phone during the day shift confirming the accusations. Even housekeeping had misgivings. What should she do? What could she do? Joe wasn't there; he was flying.

The mother manager felt she owed it to the employees who did not approve of a harlot in the establishment where they worked. Something had to be done or it would seem she approved of the bitch and her illegal profession.

Nina put a call in to the airport, stating it was an emergency from Joe Campbell's motel. They patched

her in to his plane. She told him a call girl was solic-
iting in Room 136—what should she do?

"Oh. Forget it," he replied and added, "She has a
living to make just like we do; just make sure she pays
her bill."

"Yes, she paid in advance," she told her boss.

"Well then, what are you worried about? Let her
be," he asserted before he signed off on the call.

Nina tapped her pencil repeatedly on the switchboard and thought about all the employees who called
her resenting the presence of the dirty woman and the
young personnel who didn't want to work with this
existing factor. She quickly decided what to do. She
owed it to the help who looked up to her to be caring about everything decent and righteous, and the
hell with Joe Campbell, their playboy boss—he didn't
give a shit about anything but himself and his goddamned airplane.

"This is the management. The time is now eleven
o'clock. We are aware of your solicitation in our motel
room. You have until twelve noon to check out before
I call the police and you will be in big trouble": this is
what Nina proclaimed on the telephone to the harlot
in Room 136 to resolve her dilemma.

"Don't you think I have nice legs?" asked the
woman as she walked by the front desk accompanied
by her pimp, who carried her luggage, as she lifted her
skirt, kicked up one leg, and strode her forty-some-
year-old dirty body out the front door.

Nina and the switchboard operator looked at one
another and began laughing uncontrollably. "Son of a
bitch, what a pig!" Nina managed to say and continued laughing with her coworker throughout the day.

When Joe came in later that day and was told the prostitute was gone, he simply shrugged his shoulders and didn't say a word. Nina was in charge. He loved his airplane. The motel employees thought their manager was great.

Chapter Eight

The Airplane

Joe was performing one work function on his own but decided to give this task to Nina since she was so good at everything else. The bar/lounge did not open until 11:00 A.M., just before lunch, so Joe ran off the receipts of the night before on the register and emptied the cash drawer of its monies, a task he dreaded because it was an every day chore—seven days a week. He wanted to be free to fly.

So, he taught Nina to take over these daily duties, demanding that she come in on Saturdays, Sundays, and holidays—there were to be no more days off. Joe also insisted that should she go out to dinner or a party or wherever and be gone for some time that she call in to the motel and leave a phone number where she could be reached at all times. She was in charge of everything at the motel now—Joe was free to fly any time.

Well, it was not long before Nina discovered the bar register figures did not match the bank deposits. Now what? Should she confront Joe? Should she report to his brother?

She did nothing. She waited. She kept on checking

and kept track of the amounts in discrepancy. When she was certain of obvious theft, she thought perhaps her husband might help with her decision of how to handle this problem—it was truly a heavy weight on her young mind.

Her husband listened but didn't say much. "It's up to you," was his response. He had enough on his mind with his job, working seven days a week in his trucking business. Besides, he was not in favor of his wife having such a responsible seven-days-a-week job. He remembered giving her an okay to work at the motel only part time, yet knowing how much she loved her work, he could not take that away from her.

Coming to the realization that perhaps she could be blamed for the differences between bank deposits and bar tape totals, her husband made her aware of this possibility. Agreeing that this might happen, she finally decided it was time to call Guy Campbell in Oregon before matters got worse and out of control.

She was hesitant to state the reason for her call (just like a woman, whereas, a man would just blurt it out) until Guy said, "Come on Nina, you wouldn't be calling if something wasn't wrong."

After a few sighs and some lip biting, she said, "Your brother is stealing from you."

"How do you know?" asked Guy, somewhat stunned.

"Because the bank deposits are short of the cash register receipts in the bar. It's been going on for a long time," she told him.

She was trying to be tough, not to cry as women do. She was shaking, and then the tears released due to the stress of snitching on his brother, not knowing if she was doing the right thing. After all, they were brothers, and blood is thicker than water.

Yet, Nina deemed, *If I were a man I would be thinking, fuck the son of a bitch—he is a thief. He doesn't care about the motel, just his goddamned airplane. Stealing is not right. I would never steal. How dare the shithead think he could get away with this right under my nose, the no-good bastard!*

"Okay, I'm glad you called to tell me. Don't say a word. Just go on and do the fine job you are doing. I'll be coming in soon and I'll take care of it."

This was the end of their conversation after he thanked her and she said she was sorry to relate such bad tidings about his brother.

Nina was relieved. The load shifted from her shoulders. She might now be able to sleep nights. The goddamned playboy will get his in the end. Everyone in the motel is honest; why can't he be the same? Who the hell does he think he is?

Well, then it was reported to the motel matriarch that Jenny, the young waitress servicing the pool area, was giving away free food and drink. Her friends who came to swim at the pool were not being charged for shakes, sodas, or ice cream. It was summertime. The pool was Olympic size.

Very few room rental guests made use of the pool during daytime hours. At nightfall it was enjoyed until 10:00 P.M. with much comradery among elder guests—with the help of liquor consumption, of course.

An ad in the local paper announced that for a small fee local neighbors could use the pool. Children under the age of sixteen had to be accompanied by a parent. For a $10.00 fee, a "Swim Room" was available to parents as a room to change clothes in, with instructions not to disturb the beds nor use the shower. Checkout time was 4:00 P.M. for these rooms, in time to honor reservations for incoming guests. Renting a room twice in one day brought in additional revenues.

The daytime restaurant hostess reported to Nina after much speculation that Jenny was not adding some food and drink items to the order form. Coffee, ice cream, and sodas were not ordered through the kitchen—all waitresses filled these orders themselves.

Jenny learned she could easily get away with this deceit—she left these items off the bill. However, all food orders were accounted for by the hostess, who balanced the written orders against the cash in the drawer at the end of each shift. The observant daytime hostess noticed no account for refrigerated items on the receipts from the pool, yet she saw Jenny filling plastic containers with shakes, ice cream, and sodas. No glass was allowed in the pool area.

Jenny wore her long blonde hair in a ponytail, with shorts, a blouse, and an apron that had two big pockets in front like carpenters wear. These pockets held her tip money along with the monies she pocketed from persons who did pay for confections.

Nina told Joe. Joe said, "Fire her," and walked away.

Nina thought, *No, you bastard, that's too easy.*

She chose to talk to Jenny. She told her she would have a police record at the age of seventeen unless she agreed to replace all the money she stole.

Well, there was no question as to her decision. As the friends came for more free goodies at the pool,

Jenny was ready, naming the amount owed her for all the past freebees.

They paid up. Jenny paid up. An agreeable amount of $10.00 per week out of her paycheck replaced the money that was taken. She learned a lesson. She would never forget how Nina set her on her new course of honesty, glad that her parents were spared the embarrassment she was now suffering.

A long time ago, the manager of a Woolworth dime store and an officer of the law treated a young girl harshly when she was caught stealing. They held her in the store, crying and trembling, until the parents were summoned. Nina was a witness to this, feeling no one should experience this pain, and she was glad she took care of the matter of Jenny her way.

The help smiled at Nina and thought she was the best manager a motel could have. She saved Jenny's ass. Jenny kept her job all that summer.

Joe was glad to retrieve the losses. He wished he was as cool as his manager, who really took the time to care about the motel and all its employees. He loved his airplane.

Then the robberies began. Upon reading newspaper reports of robberies in the area, Nina issued orders to the desk staff on all shifts that the motel safe combination need never be set on locked. She felt that if a gun was put to an employee's head he or she would be too frightened to remember the numbers to open the safe, and his or her life would be at risk.

It was rare that any of the guests placed valuables in the safe; they were mostly traveling salesmen coming to this industrial area or just anybodies passing through.

Joe never knew of this order. Why should he even care—they were insured. Only the motel room rental cash for the day was in the safe until the Brink's daily pickup service came.

A night auditor was needed for weekend work only. This was the 12:00 to 8:00 A.M. shift. Nina's husband's best friend asked for the job one night when they were out to dinner together.

The very first night, Ted, who was the image of Dick Tracy in the comic strips, fortyish in age and very handsome, began his part-time job for extra money. He and Ben, the night desk clerk/auditor who was doing the training, were confronted by a masked gunman who tied them up and had them lay on the floor in the back room while he took the day's receipts of around twelve hundred dollars. Most of the charges were on American Express and Visa.

The safe was open as instructed for safety of the employees. The Southtown Motel had easy access to the expressway for a fast getaway. The crook got away. Frank and Ted were somewhat shook up, but they were men, and men do not frighten as easily as women.

Nevertheless, they were glad to be alive. Frank went on with his job. Ted's wife made him quit. They had four children. The extra money was not worth the risk.

Then Martha, the 4:00 to 12:00 P.M. desk clerk was one Saturday night holding down the desk by herself because the switchboard operator reported sick. Martha did not need a replacement. She was smart. She reeked of intelligence. Everyone else was stupid in comparison. She knew the answer to a question before you asked it. She could cover the shift by herself. In fact, she enjoyed it; no one was there to disturb her college book studies when it was quiet.

Around 10:30 P.M. a very young, short black man brandished a gun at the counter and said, "Give me the money."

"No," Martha responded as she turned to see the man with the gun standing at the counter that had shelves underneath with sundries for sale.

She went on to tell the would-be robber, "If you want the money, come and get it. I'm not going to give it to you. But, when you come in here, look over there"—she pointed to the restaurant cashier desk—"The people in the dining room will see you and know something is wrong. So, you're in trouble. If I were you, I'd get out of here fast."

Tough Martha. No way would she give in to a petty thief.

The kid took off. She took off after him down the hall. She was screaming for anyone who could hear her to call the police. Restaurant employees getting ready to close for the night stood still to wonder what the hell someone was yelling about.

Martha wanted to get his license number off his getaway car, but he ran on foot down the hall, out the rear door, and disappeared in the darkness.

She ran back to the desk, still yelling for someone to hear her and to call the police. She went to the switchboard and called them herself.

Martha felt proud. The little shit didn't get any money. She expected to get a medal, a raise, praise, a pat on the back for getting rid of the would-be robber. Instead, Nina scolded her for having done what she did. Her life was more important than the money. The safe was always left open. Let him have it—they had insurance.

"Don't you dare ever do that again," Nina admonished, shaking a finger at her, then giving her a hug saying, "I'm glad you weren't hurt."

Martha was not convinced. Should the same occasion arise she would do the same—let the mother-fucking black bastard go to work like she is and go to college, all in a day's time, too. "Shit! I deserve a raise," she thought as she pursed her lips in disappointment.

After this incident Martha was not as happy on the job as before. Most of the employees told her that she was very brave. She had saved the motel some money. They thought she should have been rewarded.

Martha harbored resentment against the motel to the point that it was hard for her to smile at guests and her coworkers. She wished she didn't need the money for car expenses, clothes, and school costs. She began complaining about the guests who had no luggage. These room rentals were called quickie/shack jobs, and she thought they should not be allowed.

When women came into the bar alone, she felt they were all prostitutes and this should be stopped.

She detested the fiftyish woman who every Wednesday afternoon rented and paid for a room on the main floor in the rear of the building, where her secret lover would sneak in, not to be seen by anyone who might know him. He was the most renowned realtor in the area and she his mistress/secretary. It was rare for a woman to sign in for a room rental, so Martha assumed it had to be hanky-panky.

The skips, as they were called (checkout rooms

who left and did not pay), really bothered Martha. She thought they should be caught and sent to jail; after all, even she had to pay room and board at home.

Nina narrated to Joe about their unhappy, complaining desk clerk. Martha was all righteous regarding all the wrongs in the business, and her depression rubbed off onto all the other coworkers. She didn't like the fact that the waitresses slept around and flirted for bigger tips and that even the motel owner had a girlfriend. Putting all her grumblings together, she assessed that she was working in a big, one-hundred-and-ten-room house of ill repute that she wished would catch on fire one day soon and burn to the ground.

She detested Tom Stevens, their handsomest steady guest who made advances to every female in the place, even Martha, wishing to bed them all. His erections were so obvious and disgusting that she wanted to puke right on him, not knowing that he felt women wanted to be treated this way; he thought that's why God put them here—to be loved by man. He was a nice guy away from home; all one had to do was laugh with him and make him feel he was special. That's all—he meant no harm—he was a beautiful man. Secretly, Martha found pleasure from Tom Stevens's attention and flattery; she even blushed and looked very pretty with pink cheeks. Everyone loves compliments, men as well as women. Yet, Martha was inundated with condemnation.

Joe listened to Nina's report about Martha and then told her how he felt about the business so that she would tell all the underlings: "They should treat it as a job. If we didn't rent to shack jobs, the other motels would get the business. What the waitresses do on their own time is their business. Tom Stevens is a steady guest and must be shown our respect. We do not have the privilege of guessing who the prostitutes are. If the guests hire them, it is their business; even the local police use them." Lastly he said, "Don't knock sex—it is here to stay," as he walked away to hurry with motel responsibilities and then go flying.

But Martha did not agree when her manager related the owner's words in answer to her queries. One day when she and Nina were scheduled to cover the desk and switchboard, Martha was a half hour late. She hurried in, dropped her books down with a loud bang, didn't say good morning or offer any excuse for being late, then finally said, "I hate this place."

Now, Nina was always in a good mood; she loved her job. She didn't mind her coworker not being on time—at least she showed up. She had many duties to perform in her workday and found it not too easy to do it alone.

Nina learned to let things be that she could not transform, yet she saw no reason why she had to work with a young lady bent upon depression due to disliking her place of employment and unable to smile at a job that required a big smile while performing a service.

"I'm going to do you a big favor, Martha," Nina resolved when she told her to pick up her books and leave. "You should find another job that suits you. This one doesn't. You are a good, smart girl. I will gladly give you a good recommendation when you need it."

After a long stare and then a deep sigh, Martha

replied, "I guess you're right." She picked up her books and left.

When Joe came in later that morning, he asked where her helper was. "She doesn't work here anymore," Nina answered unsmilingly. Joe just shrugged his shoulders and went into the dining room, looking for his new girlfriend that excited him.

Nina would have to cover the desk and switchboard that day, but without the stress of a disgruntled coworker.

Martha's father Ben, in his fifties, stocky build, square faced, was the night auditor/desk clerk who rang up all room charges on the NCR machine and totaled the day's receipts. He worked two jobs to meet the expense of sending two children through college.

Nina, the diplomat, did not want to lose Ben, because it takes a long time to train a replacement. She also knew she would have the added job of accomplishing this task by going in at 4:00 A.M. to do the work until the new person could do it alone. Management takes a risk when hiring family members, because should one be fired or quit, the other may choose to follow suit in support.

Nina chose to call Ben, whom she had just relieved of duty when she came in at 8:00 A.M. She waited until she thought Ben was at home and before Martha got home to call and tell him why she let his daughter go.

He of course was stunned, but Nina went on to relate Martha's disposition of late. Ben listened. Ben knew. He agreed. It was okay. He understood. Who better than he could know the transgressions of night people in a motel. He closed his eyes to all and did his job for the money he needed, but he was aware that everything bothered his daughter.

It wasn't long before Nina received a call from a large insurance company asking about a former employee named Martha Winters. They called back a second time to confirm the good report on an employee that was fired. "The job simply did not suit her," is what Nina repeatedly depicted in addition to many favorable attributes of her intelligence. Martha got the job.

Chapter Nine

No Good

One morning the telephone woke Nina at 6:00 A.M. The voice on the other end was that of the breakfast cook at the motel, telling her the large kitchen fan was not working and that it was going to be one hell of a hot day. With the temperature outdoors expected to be ninety degrees, the interior air in the kitchen would be in the one hundreds. It had to be fixed or else the cook might quit, food service would be uncertain, tempers would be short, and business would be lost.

Nina dressed quickly and while en route to the motel passed a sign announcing an electrical contractor that was very close to her home; she memorized the name and telephone number. When she reached the motel, she called the company, thinking since it was so close by, perhaps someone could come right away to solve the fan problem; it was really early for people to be on the job.

Well, sure enough, it so happened that the man answering the phone was just elevated from field electrician to superintendent in charge of all work. His first day on the job compelled him to get to work early to impress his boss.

Ten minutes later he responded to the urgent call and reported the fan motor needed cleaning of kitchen grease pollution or replacement. Another fan was brought in by 10:00 A.M. to save the day while the other one was getting attention.

High esteem by all befell this young man in his middle thirties. He was very handsome, six feet tall, with a brush hair cut, sparkling brown eyes, and vigor in his walk. He saved the hot day in the kitchen of the Southtown Motel.

Everybody liked him. He came for coffee and a roll in the morning and began coming for lunch with his electrical associates—one hand feeds the other. He was soon getting work orders for all electrical work at the motel.

Frequent visits looking for work and/or coffee prompted the waitresses to finally ask him his name. "Just call me No Good Bastard," was his response. He had had a bad day. Nothing was going right. He was greeted with swear words from his customers for shortcomings in the work being performed by his company field workers that morning.

So Jim Peters of Southside Electric was called "No Good" every time he came in to the motel. It stuck. He enjoyed it. He was jovial.

He took a liking to the gal with the long legs also known as Joe's new girlfriend. She excited many a man. If you were comparing waitresses, she would be considered "slinky." Her legs were long—the kind a man envisions wrapped around him while she lay under him—her hair black and curly, eyes dark brown, and white skin wearing no makeup except for fire red lipstick. She lacked substantial breasts, her bra-less nipples showing through her uniform, looking like big, loose buttons as she swished around the dining room.

It wasn't long before it was noticed that Jackie with the long legs would often say she had to go to her car—she forgot something. In the meantime, Jim Peters was already in his company van outside in the motel parking lot, waiting for her and the quick blow job to release the excitement she created in him. She returned to the restaurant in a matter of about eight minutes.

"Lightning" was Jackie's new name by all who suspected their quickie pleasures.

Joe was always flying when this fun took place and never knew.

Joe did do some work on rainy days when flying was not feasible, and he felt a little guilty not spending enough time on the job. Inventory of the kitchen supplies made him go to the motel at 11:00 P.M. one night, just before time for the cook to go off duty, to check if all was well. Well, it was not.

Roasts, steaks, and bacon were exiting the back door into the cook's car trunk. Good God! Why wasn't someone checking? Cook got fired. New cook came in and was watched.

No wonder Harry and Louie Katz never took their eyes off anything when they were in charge; everyone needs supervision and must answer to some-one to stay honest. Joe was learning that a motel owner cannot afford to even sleep. "What a fucking business!" he thought, wishing he could fly more.

Chapter Ten

Damien

Then there was the night bartender. The day bartender couldn't possibly do anything wrong; there were too many bosses on duty—owner, manager, and hostess—too many eyes everywhere. However, the night bartender worked from 6:00 P.M. to 4:00 A.M. This was a different story.

Karen, the night dining room hostess, called Nina at home one Saturday night to tell her of the corrupt night bartender and his exploits.

Damien was immaculate in his white shirt, black tie, and black pants. His thin mustache was perfectly trimmed, his hair black and sleek. He was forever rolling and rerolling his shirt sleeves up to the elbows as he talked, moved, and even when en route to the bathroom.

This nervous manner hid his mischievous habits to gain money from the fools surrounding his trade. This extra money enabled him to supply his gorgeous wife with diamonds, furs, dresses, and household furnishings and his two kids with whatever they wished. While you were watching him rolling his sleeves, his eyes were everywhere, looking for means to fill his pockets with cash besides tending bar.

He had a brick fence surrounding his house and property to protect everything. His residence was the most impressive in his modest neighborhood—it is impressive what money will buy, especially when attained in addition to a working paycheck.

Karen respected Nina's honesty and integrity in managing the motel with its many misdemeanors, corruptions, and discrepancies. Well, oh my God, another time for Nina to speculate how to handle this shit. Karen had called her from her apartment when she got home from work late at night.

Nina was now apprised of the bartender, Damien, doing his thing against the management and getting away with it. He had been there for years, and he had been getting away with it for years. He was slick. He even had Harry and Louie Katz fooled—that's how slick he was.

It was different now. The help had someone who cared to tell it to in hopes it would be stopped, because right was right and wrong was wrong. How dare he continue to get away with it? Nina was here.

If Karen had told Joe Campbell, the playboy left in charge, the shithead who could not care less about anything, what the bartender was doing, it was felt he would act hastily. He would insist on naming names, let Damien be aware he had enemies, take away Damien's livelihood and all the goodies he was used to for years, and get informants killed. So much for those thoughts; this quandary required someone acting with smarts to catch a thief or else there would be hell to pay.

So Nina said nothing until late one Saturday night around 9:30 P.M. She telephoned Joe at his home and told him there was an urgent motel matter and that she must see him. She realized that if she chose to tell him all during working hours, Joe would be hasty in firing Damien, name many persons, and be a jerk, not caring about the consequences to others involved.

It was 10:00 P.M. when Nina rang the bell of Joe's house. They had company. The children were asleep. Joe excused himself from his guests, and they went out on the enclosed downstairs patio to talk where they could not be heard. His house in the suburbs was a trilevel.

Nina's purpose in this late night meeting, as she related to her employer, was that she did not wish for him to be hasty in his decision after she told him everything or many persons would be hurt. She wanted him to sleep on the information.

"Huh" and "Okay" were his responses after she related her story. He had to get back to his guests. She left and prayed her boss would handle things the right way for the sake of many.

Damien, as reported by Karen, was having a woman friend bring in bottles of cheap liquor to add to similar bottles to replace what Damien was pocketing and not ringing up in the motel bar cash register. This was accomplished after all employees went home. This is why inventory always made him look good, with no suspicion of cheating on bar liquor sales. Oh, he was slick. Nina told Joe this. "Hmm," Joe hummed in disbelief.

Another report was that Damien, while nervously rolling up his shirt sleeves, would go behind the desk to look at the register of rooms and ask for a key to an "on change" room so that he would not have to use the motel washroom.

"On change" rooms, and there were usually one, two, or more, meant guests could leave their luggage in their room and check out late. They were asked not to disturb the cleaned room and were not charged for another day.

These rooms had to be checked before renting to new guests. If there were enough rooms to fill reservations, these rooms stayed on change until the next day when housekeeping came on duty. If the room was suddenly needed, the bellhop would be assigned to check the room before rental and put it in order.

Fridays were the heaviest late checkout days due to some steady weekly guests having to work all day on Fridays. Steady guests were privileged in this respect with hopes of a return visit.

Damien would take the key to one of these rooms on the pretext it was for his personal hygiene usage, except he was acting as liaison pimp between men and call girls. He pocketed the money for the room rental fee and his share of the fee for the prostitute he contacted from the neighboring bars where they hung out, waiting for a call.

The son of a bitch was getting a fee for the room, a percentage of the prostitute fee, and making more money than the motel did for one night's room rental by also pocketing liquor sales.

Joe was vexed. Nina was good. She was the mother. She was trusted by all to do the right thing. Everyone worked for a living. How dare anyone get away with evil and make money illegally and get away with it? His time would come.

Thank God she went to Joe at night so that he could sleep on it. Do not be hasty, Joe. People will be blamed. Damien will lose his job. His wife will miss her goodies with his easy money.

Nina asked that if he was to let Damien go, to do it for another reason other than what she had told him.

All Joe did was shake his head back and forth. He said not a word to his guests nor to his wife that evening about the visit from his motel manager. Joe wondered, when Nina took her leave, how in the hell she could learn so much about the affairs at his motel when he knew nothing—it was inconceivable.

She was on the job more than Joe, that's how. She was intelligent and caring, loved what she was doing, and asked all the help to report to her any suspicions, large or small, of wrongdoing. She did nothing about misconduct until she was certain of the charges and took deep breaths until resolved that she was doing the right thing.

Joe did wait, taking his manager's advice of sleeping on it. He decided Nina was right—persons could be hurt, even he or his family.

One morning, weeks later, the kitchen was in disarray at 6:00 A.M. when Joe was called and advised that the morning cook would be late for work due to a flat tire on his car. Joe had no choice but to cover the duties of cooking until the cook could get there.

When Joe entered the kitchen, it was not tidy, as it should have been after each shift. He saw a pile of dirty dishes, pots and pans, and silverware that had been used and not washed and placed in their proper place, ready for the next shift.

"Hmmmm, we'll see about this," was all he could say. He said it out loud; however, no one was there to hear him. The waitresses were busy with their chores before opening the restaurant to their motel guests, yet they waited with bended ear to hear an outburst of anger from the kitchen—they saw the mess before Joe arrived.

Damien had not gone home as yet. He was still in the bar, much to Joe's surprise. Joe questioned his night bartender about the mess in the kitchen. Damien admitted he was guilty of entertaining intoxicated friends of his who became hungry at 5:00 A.M. He stated that they spent a great deal of money on liquor in the motel bar, and he could not refuse their request for food before they got into their respective cars to head for home.

Well, as far as Joe was concerned, this was theft and disrespect in the workplace.

Joe fired Damien for this reason and no other reason, making no mention of his practices regarding call girls, room rentals, and phony liquor inventory. Whew! That was over. Joe continued flying. Nina did her job of running his motel.

A female bartender was hired. Jim thought a woman might be more trustworthy in this type of work, yet decided to check on the night shift often.

Chapter Eleven

The Lie

Alice Campbell grew more and more suspicious that her husband had a girlfriend to go flying with him because she would not. He was going up more than ever before.

One Saturday, Nina was at the desk. She stopped in on a day off to see if all was well, knowing the desk clerk was working alone and the switchboard operator was sick. She answered the switchboard when it buzzed. It was Alice asking for Joe. "He's not here," Nina replied.

Alice asked, "Do you know where he is?"

"He went flying about one o'clock," Nina responded.

"Who did he go with?"

"He might have gone with Mike, the houseboy."

"Are you sure?"

"Well, no, except that Mike left shortly after your husband did."

"Huh. I'll bet he went flying with his girlfriend."

"Oh, I don't know about that."

"I'm going to go to the airport with my kids and

catch them together." Alice decided this was her chance to affirm her suspicions.

Nina gasped, "Oh my God, don't do that. You are imagining things. You are upset. Don't go there with the kids. If you insist on going there, bring the kids to my house. I'm leaving right now—I'll be home. I'll take care of them. It's a long ride to the airport—it's forty-five minutes away."

Alice did not take her advice. She said, "No, no, I'm going," and hung up, breaking the connection and leaving Nina in utter dismay and wondering: *What now?*

The next day was Sunday. For some unknown reason the Sunday newspaper was not delivered to Nina's house. She and her husband drove to the motel at about 1:00 P.M. that day in hopes of finding a newspaper to purchase, because the drug store in their area was sold out—the church crowd got them.

Joe saw Nina enter the lobby, called her into the office, and fired her for getting involved in the personal life of his wife and family.

When Alice and the children arrived at the airport in Gary, Indiana, she had the tower radio her husband and announce that they were waiting for his return. This was something she had never, ever, done before. Even the airport personnel were wondering why she and the children were there—and on a Saturday?

It was almost an hour later that Joe and Mike landed.

When Alice saw no girlfriend, she decided to play on her husband's sympathy and not look the jealous fool. Hysterically, she began crying. Joe comforted her. The children began crying because their mother was crying. Mike stood back, wondering what the heck was happening. In between sobs, gum chewing/cracking, and blowing her nose, she told her husband that when she called the motel asking for him, Nina told her that if she went to the airport she could catch her husband with another woman. Her tears increased, then subsided, another stick of gum went into her mouth, and she gave a deep sigh before looking up at her husband.

She was proud of her performance, knowing Joe loved his kids and felt they should be at home right then and not there. How dare Nina do this to his family? Joe was saying his usual "Hmmm" and thinking he would set things right so that it would never happen again.

So Alice got her wish, knowing if Nina was gone her husband could not find as much time to go flying—motel duties were numerous. "Ha, ha, I fixed her and him," was the gum chewer's conviction. She had longed for the opportunity, and it arrived as though she had planned it. Did you ever see a pretty woman chew gum and smile widely at the same time? The shrew! A pretty woman turned ugly due to her unfounded jealousies.

Nina had tried to defend herself against the lie when Joe told her his wife blamed her for her hysteria and upset children on a beautiful Saturday afternoon, but of course Joe believed his wife, and that was that.

He said, "Good-bye. I will mail your check," without even looking up at her.

She turned and left in disbelief that this could happen to her when she was so devoted to his motel and its work. There was nothing she could do. She was convicted of an untruth.

It was Nina's turn to shed some tears. She had loved her job of eight years. She enjoyed seeing people from all over the world, even Japan and as far away as Australia, who patronized the motel, visiting the Simmons Company home office mattress plant that was in the area. She was fond of all the help who looked up to her as their boss.

Joe was a nothing playboy who thought of no one other than himself. He was envious of the respect Nina had from everyone, but her work permitted him to come and go as he pleased. He had to hire three people to take her place.

Two days later she called Jim's brother, Guy, and told him tearfully what happened.

Guy Campbell came in the following week. He was told Joe's side of the story and then went to Nina's home to hear hers. Being the gentleman that Guy was, he said nothing against his sister-in-law; she was his brother's wife, and he wanted peace in the family. However, knowing what a loss Nina was to the motel, he told her he would do whatever she wished. He would force her on Joe if she chose to keep her job.

Well, she did not want to do that, and her husband agreed. Many thanks were exchanged, and also good-byes.

Guy would miss the gal who ratted on his brother for stealing restaurant funds. Honesty is treasured. Nina was a treasure. When Guy confronted his brother about the cash discrepancies, Joe told him he needed the money for repairs to his expensive airplane at the time. Joe said he intended to replace the money he took.

Guy felt he owed his manager an explanation. When he told her, she just nodded her head and thought, *Oh yeah? Joe, you lying son of a bitch! If I didn't catch ya, you would probably keep it up . . . you and your goddamned airplane. Why don't you work like the rest of us do? You selfish, spoiled rotten brat!* She wanted to instead say "rotten bastard!" That's how she felt about the vice president of the motel she loved working in.

That evening Nina received a call from Oregon. It was Guy's wife, Joan, who knew what a lying, troublemaking, jealous woman Alice always was. Joan had had numerous confrontations with her sister-in-law, who enjoyed finding fault with others, thinking this would make her look better.

It was very unfortunate. Alice was a very pretty woman. Her children were beautiful. Joan wanted Nina to know she was on her side against the gum-chewing bitch who finally found a way to hurt her own husband in hopes he could not fly as much. She did not realize how much she hurt her husband's motel operation and its efficiency.

It was a hardship on Nina to suddenly find herself at home after so many years of doing something she really enjoyed. She missed her fifty-dollar tipper who came in once a week for a room to be used for a short time in the afternoon, a room that would be cleaned and ready again for rental that evening. He would enter the restaurant, have a cup of coffee, and Nina, after acknowledging that he was there, took him the key. He did not register; Nina did it for him. This procedure was an irregularity, but who knows if people use fictitious names rather than real in cases such as this? What did it matter if they paid in advance?

She never asked any questions. She learned throughout her motel education that some people cannot love openly; they must hide and make love not to hurt anyone. This elderly man was immaculate in a starched white shirt, expensive cuff links, diamond ring, black striped suit, and shiny shoes. He carried a cane for his walk with a limp, which gave him the appearance of a gentleman personified.

She never saw his secret love. On one of these encounters when he had time to talk and Nina had time to listen, she learned he had a very profitable company and now his two sons were taking him to court, claiming he was incompetent to govern his company. His pain was only felt by himself and his secretary, who understood what his wife did not. He was trying to keep his self-esteem after all the years of hard work, not wanting to feel worthless in his elder years.

The love of the woman he was joining here was helping him keep his desire to live on.

Sure, Nina took care of all wrongdoings at the motel, but when it came to matters of the heart she had a respect for love and knew it to be stronger than money, heaven, or hell. Love—the most tremendous force of all.

She even understood Tom Stevens's behavior when he fell in love with one of the pretty faces that was a conquest. He always left for home on Fridays, but one weekend he stayed over.

"What are you doing here?" Nina asked him, surprised to see him at the motel on a Saturday.

"Oh, Nina, I'm in love. I'm no good. I'm a bastard. I know I should go home. I will," he said as he hung his head low yet smiled with guilt.

"Go home to your wife and kids. You're all mixed up. You're a good guy, but you are too handsome; that's what gets you in trouble."

"I know. You're right. I'm bad," he said and walked away.

Sometimes those who fool around make good husbands because of their guilt. One month later, in the summertime, Tom brought his lovely wife and children on his trip to Chicago, introduced them to everyone, and from then on always went home on Fridays.

Perhaps he was getting older and had had enough complications of the heart. Was it worth it? Hell no. Women always want to win, want to possess, and need commitment—so different from a man's needs, in search of fulfilling their ego and an enormous sex drive.

Chapter Twelve

Nina

Nina missed people. The motel had been an adventure, an education better than college. Her husband wished he could buy the place for her; he knew how much she loved it. He gave her comfort and strength by saying, "The hell with Joe. You are his loss." He encouraged her to relax and take a long rest and also said, "Sometimes things happen for the best."

He reminded her of all she had learned while on the job—all phases of bookkeeping, payroll, handling money, reports, using a calculator and typewriter, and best of all, diplomatically supervising people. She could easily get a job elsewhere when she was ready. She had had a great education on the job and learned more than any school could have taught her, because she had some outstanding attributes—common sense, a feeling of "do unto others as you would have others do unto you," and a great, genuine smile that exhibited her love of people.

Her husband took her and their son on a two-week Caribbean cruise. The long rest made her remember her lifelong dream of one day completing her book that she later titled *1234 5th Avenue,* the address she and her sister made up. All the houses where they lived picked up their mail at the post office as there was no delivery service available.

She began putting her notes together for her book regarding her life on a small farm with her Russian family.

A few months later she had to put them away when the doorbell rang and a very handsome man who knew her from the motel came to ask her to work for him.

She began in her home, because the electrical contractor was just beginning and had no office as yet. She applied all she had learned at the motel and handled all his paperwork, money, and bookkeeping. Her book had to wait.

Oh my God! She realized that she was working for "No Good Bastard," the very handsome, virile, jovial, vigor-in-his-step young man who quickened his pleasure with "Lightning" periodically, even in broad daylight.

His company grew, and he rented an office and shop. She was his CFO, with a salary equal to an executive man in her position. She managed his office and all monies, payroll, accounts payable and receivable, and union reports and payments. She also hired all the help to assist her while she paid the taxes and had everything ready to prepare financial statements annually.

The boss did his part by bringing in the work, never having to worry about the office and its many functions. He believed in hiring self-motivated people and surrounded himself with them. Nina revered her most generous boss and loved her job. "Sometimes things happen for the best," she remembered someone telling her not too long ago. She was now earning five times more than the motel had paid her.

When the company was doing well, the Christmas bonuses put smiles on all faces. Nina's amount matched that given to the two project managers; after all, she was his controller—meeting all dollar needs to keep the company alive. What a challenge! She couldn't wake early enough to shower, exercise, and be on the job by 7:30 A.M. Her scheduled working hours were 8:00 A.M. to 5:00 P.M. daily, five days a week, but many times she got there earlier and stayed later and even went in on Saturdays. She had to be on top of everything; he was paying her well, and the responsibilities were extensive.

One day one of the project managers entered her office to gossip sheepishly to her about their boss. "Guess what?" John Golden said as he stood in front of her desk. His job was reading blueprints regarding the submission of bids on new buildings or revisions to existing buildings, commercial and/or industrial.

Nina looked up and shrugged her shoulders, not saying the anticipated response of "What?"

John announced smugly what was supposed to be a secret among men only: "Our boss has a girlfriend."

Secrets do not stay secrets very long. Now Nina knew.

"How do you know?" he was asked.

"He just now told me," John announced gleefully, almost laughingly. "Her name is Jeannie, and she works at Acme Steel where we are doing electrical repairs."

Nina just shook her head side to side before he turned and left her office. She said not a word, questioning why a coworker would come to tell her this and wondering why her boss would tell another man something so personal. Perhaps men enjoy boasting of such conquests.

Everyone in the office knew that John Golden had a girlfriend. For some reason, he enjoyed the fact that this was known. John was in his forties, medium build, still with a full head of hair and a nice friendly smile. He was a married man with one child, but his extracurricular activities included sexually engaging another woman on the side for many years. In fact, this was his third extramarital partner, and he announced the affairs to all his coworkers and to anyone who would listen.

My God! Nina thought, *What a jerk! Affairs should be a secret.* She remembered having told her husband that should he have an affair, not to tell her; she did not want to know, no matter what. She resolved that should she experience the same, she would tell no one, not even her mother, and she told her mother everything. Illicit intimacy should be a universal accredited lie—in other words, keep the shit to yourself.

So, Nina concluded that by John telling her of the boss now having a girlfriend, he felt he wasn't the only guilty one committing sin. John's extra and now Jim Peter's extra were calling the office often, announcing the guilt of the two men.

When a travel agent called to confirm the itinerary for a Sun Valley four-day stay for Mr. and Mrs. Jim Peters, Jim told Nina where he was going. Should a company emergency arise, she had to know how and where to get in touch with her boss.

Lo and behold, his wife, Tina, and daughter, Angel,

came to the office the next day after he left on his trip, and Nina had to close her aghast open mouth to hide her realization that it was not his wife in Vegas with him but his new plaything. The goddamned son of a bitch was really screwing around dangerously. He told his wife he was going with a cousin.

Tina was a size sixteen, tall, but not too tall, brunette with very short hair, almost boyish, yet quite attractive, with a square face. She wore little makeup and was most friendly to everyone and well liked. And Angel was as cute as cute can be.

This deceit continued. Jeannie called Jim every day. Nina was concerned. Once again, she saw a handsome man, irresistible to women, with a grandiose ego, bragging to his fellow barstool buddies, who in return boasted about their sexual triumphs. Each had a wife and children.

This was just playing around. They had no intention of hurting anyone, especially their families whom they loved very much. They were getting away with fun and games on the side—so what? A piece of ass was just a piece of meat to enjoy because that was how man was made. How could something that feels so good be so bad? Just don't let the wife find out or there will be hell to pay.

Excitement heals boredom. Sexual fulfillment makes a man sleep like a baby. These thoughts were perceived by men who fooled around, enjoying these pleasures.

Once again there was the trip to Las Vegas. Mr. and Mrs. Jim Peters spent a week sunning, swimming, golfing, screwing, and deceiving the people back home into thinking he was there for a new job to be bid on.

Oh well, just another excursion. He was having fun away from home—just don't hurt anyone, especially the children who needed him.

All this togetherness was leading Jeannie to feel possessive of her lover. "Leave her," were her often-spoken words.

"I can't—the kids," was his rebuttal—he had three. "Wait until they're grown, then we can be together." He held her in abatement and continued his exciting activities, with his wife and family unaware of his infidelity.

A seven-day cruise was being planned for the springtime. Jim had to make a decision—should he take his wife or his girlfriend? The determining factor was that three cousins and their wives were going along on this trip; the cousins planned it. Well, there was no way he was going to take Jeannie. She was a secret. It was not time to bring her out into the open. He had no intention of this at this time anyway. He loved his wife. He loved his children. He also loved his cousins; they were close from childhood. He cared what his family thought of him. To expose this situation now would mean divorce, and the thought of it never crossed his mind as yet. In fact, it frightened him whenever Jeannie mentioned it.

He told her he was taking his wife on the cruise with his beloved cousins and their wives. Well, she was very indignant. She asked him what happened to all the "I love you" words exchanged. "Will you marry me?" she would ask often.

"In a minute," he always responded.

This ultimatum was declared by Jeannie regarding the anticipated cruise: "I'll give you one week to reconsider."

No response from Jim. This was it. He pondered. How much did she mean to him? Just fun and games forever after? What about the kids? What about the cousins? What about the company people? He hadn't expected this. She knew he was a married man. He was not free. Why the hell couldn't things go on as they were? It was fun. It was stimulating. He wasn't ready to leave his wife.

One week before the scheduled cruise, with no change of heart from her lover, at 11:00 P.M. on a Monday night, Jeannie rang the doorbell of Jim's home. After four rings Jim's wife Tina went to the door with her daughter following her. They found Jeannie (whom they had never met) at the door, holding a folded piece of paper and announcing, "I think you should have this." She handed it to Tina, turned away, walked to her car, and drove off.

Tina was dumbfounded. Who was this woman? What was this piece of paper? What the heck was going on? Her daughter Angel sleepily asked, rubbing her eyes, "Mom, what is it?"

"I don't know. Let's see," Tina responded. She went to turn on more lights in the house, enabling her to read the paper given to her by a young woman with brown hair and brown eyes, not too attractive, slight in build, and flat chested.

"What is this all about?" Tina said out loud. She was thinking someone had the wrong house.

The blaring lights in the living room where her daughter and now two sons gathered after being wakened by the ringing door bell enabled Tina to read a statement from a Las Vegas hotel. It showed Mr. and Mrs. Jim Peters having registered in Room 816 for the week of April 7, 1970, and listed all the charges to room, restaurant, and bar.

Jim slept through this visit by his lover to his family, because he had entertained an account at lunch, and having consumed heavy amounts of liquor that afternoon, he was now sound asleep. Tina cried. The two teenage boys swore and went back to bed. The daughter stayed close to her mother and said not a word. It was too much for her to grasp; she was only ten.

The next morning the children exited for school. Tina showed Jim the hotel receipt and told him about the young woman who brought it to their door late the night before. She told her husband that the children were also aware of the deceit.

This time she did not shed tears. She just waited for his response—there was none. He was too stunned. He left the house and went to his job. Jim realized he had been caught. How dare the bitch hurt his family; they were a separate life from her.

He had to wait until the end of the day when Jeannie would be home from her job to confront her with what she had done.

Jim was in her apartment, having had a key, even before she got home. He was pacing the floors, building up his anger based upon the inconceivable act of hurting him and his family just because he was not ready for divorce and would not take her on the cruise with his cousins. They meant more to him than she did, he realized finally.

Her entrance and one look at her face, which by this time made him aware that she was one jealous bitch, led him to attack. Not wanting to injure her, he chose to break every picture, table, and dish, upturn every piece of loose furnishing in her apartment, swear profusely, and ask why she did what she had done, without waiting for an answer. He looked back before exiting the door, making certain everything was destroyed. How dare the plaything do this to his family? She was a nothing. The affair was over. He loved his family more.

Jim tried to explain his foolishness. He begged forgiveness. He promised never to do this again—the girl meant nothing to him. Tina chose to yield, thinking of the children who adored their father. Jim, Tina, and the cousins and their wives went on the cruise.

But it was very hard for Tina to forget. They had been high school sweethearts—first love for both. She began concentrating on her children more, their needs, school and extracurricular activities necessitating her to not be home when time for her husband to be home for dinner. Dinner was not ready. His clothes were not ironed. The house was not tidy. Their arguments were fierce and became habitual.

The children took sides, of course against the father. They were knowledgeable of the hotel receipt proving infidelity against their mother and could not forget it. The two boys, fourteen and seventeen years in age, kept to their rooms. The girl could not look at her father nor go near him, finding it difficult to cope with this terrible happening in their family.

Now, Nina was Jim's confidant, his right arm in all matters in the workplace. Yet not in all the years of her employment with him did he mention his personal life to her. He had never said anything derogatory against his wife or children. They were such a happy family that Nina felt they never had any problems.

A great number of months passed, when one day Jim and Nina had to meet with attorneys regarding nonpayment of an account. On their way back to the office from the Chicago Loop they were stopped in traffic on the Dan Ryan Expressway. After having exhausted their conversation concerning the purpose of their trip, there was quiet time, allowing Jim to reflect upon his personal problems. He began relating in detail the story of what Jeannie had done to hurt him and his family.

Nina was aware that her boss had a girlfriend because her telephone calls to the office were numerous, almost daily. Nina just listened and shook her head in disbelief, not offering any solutions to his grief. She took great pride in the fact that her boss trusted her enough as a friend to be able to talk about personal matters. She felt he and his family must be suffering greatly.

A few months later, Jim telephoned Nina, who was already in bed for the evening. He needed a friend to talk to. He was sobbing and found it rather hard to speak. Nina questioned what was wrong, and he finally told her he left home but that he really did not want to. He admitted he was scared and didn't know where to go or what to do. He said he could no longer live under the same roof with his wife. He was truly anguished.

What could Nina offer? Do what you must do?

Go home and try to work it out? What about the children? What do you want? She mentioned all points, ending by telling him if there was anything she could do not to hesitate to ask.

Chapter Thirteen

Jim

Jim moved into an apartment close to his office. He and his wife remained separated for a year before she filed for divorce, after finally realizing he was not going to return home. She thought he would; after all, they had been married for eighteen years and had three children and a basically good life with much laughter and love.

However, now it was all changed. Tina could not erase what he had done to deceive her and his children, but she hoped her husband would beg to come home; there would be no other man for her than him.

But Jim was now enjoying being free. He was a good cook, so food was no problem for him. His shirts now went to the very best cleaners in town to be perfectly starched to his liking. All controversies that angered him to daily headaches before were eliminated. Yet he missed his beautiful home with the swimming pool and the best of landscaping and decor inside and outside—the comfort he had worked so hard for with the success of his company.

The house was near his country club and many friends and accounts that he thoroughly enjoyed and treasured. He thought they had the best of everything, and now it meant nothing because he was not a happy man and his wife was not a happy woman. His children hated him for leaving their mother.

The women came in droves. It was easy for him. He was so handsome. All he had to say was, "Let's go to bed," and they gladly accepted. He met them for lunch. He met them for dinner. Some even came to the office. He bedded all of them.

He impressed them by announcing he was president of his company. He used his appeal to the fullest and enjoyed every minute of it. Most of them wanted a commitment.

He compared them to his wife, who just lay there performing her duty, while these women crawled all over him. When he sat on the barstool with his buddies, he had sexual experiences to relate that astounded his men friends who were also active in this respect. None could compare—he had more to tell than they. You see, they were still married, and he was free.

Nina knew her boss was screwing everything available to him. She heard many a female voice asking for him on the telephone, prompting her to tell him he had better get himself fixed or else there could be a paternity claim against him and the corporation. He listened and released a long "hummm."

The following week when she went into his office, he was not seated. He was standing behind his executive chair talking on the telephone. When he hung the phone on its cradle Nina asked, "Why don't you sit down?"

Jim grinned and replied, "I can't. I took your advice."

"Good," Nina responded with a big grin and added, "Hurts, huh?"

"Yep."

The AIDS disease came into play, arousing fear in all who were promiscuous. This meant to Jim that he had better find a permanent partner. He was fearful due to his loose conduct with so many women; besides, he liked being married, having a home to go to and all the comforts associated with everyday living.

His divorce was final. Nina was called into many meetings with Tina's lawyers, who demanded financial statements on the corporation.

Tina got all personal possessions, such as house, car, furniture. She was fair in giving Jim what he asked for. She sold the house in the elaborate country club area, bought a smaller one, and the children remained with her. Alimony was thirty-five hundred dollars per month for 8 years. He gladly paid just to be done with that part of his life.

Tina still loved him and thought he would return to her and the kids.

He never did. "Why should I live like that when I can live like this?" was his resolve. He still loved his wife, but he could not live with her is what he told Nina.

Along came another late night telephone call from her boss, who was sobbing on the other end. Now what? Well, the AIDS scare led him to an attractive woman ten years his junior. She was a divorcée with three children. Her husband left her for another woman.

Jim had been dating her and then bedding her

until she asked for a package marriage, meaning her children came along with her. Well, he was past having children—especially someone else's children. He did not like her son nor her two daughters; they were too scholarly, too spoiled, too serious. He compared them to his own, who were just the opposite—they were more fun-loving, loving, and cheerful, just like their father.

He was sobbing because he broke up with her, telling Nina all the details. Once again, what could she say to him? I can understand? Think of yourself? You have to be happy? There are a lot of fish in the sea? Hang in there, the right one will come along?

She said all of the above—what else could she say? It was his life. She was just a friendly listening ear; however, she wanted him to be happy.

He was a great guy with a big generous heart who deserved a contented life.

He moved in with the divorcee into her house after realizing her children were teenagers and would soon be leaving the nest. The boy would be going off to college the next year and the twin girls in two; besides, it wasn't easy to find a woman in her forties who had no children—most of his dates had four, and one redhead he really flipped for had six. Well, there was no way he could handle that life. So he succumbed to the best available offer in his desperation to live a quiet life as he once did and have a home to go to every night. He was an old-fashioned man, and he was afraid to continue his dangerous ways. She would have to do.

"Tell your new landlady to take good care of you

or I'll beat the shit out of her," is what Nina said to her boss when he announced his new telephone number and address to his employees.

"I will," is all he said without smiling, still wondering if he made the right decision.

They married. The reception was held at her country club. She was so snobbish that she did not even socialize with her new husband's employees and their wives or husbands who were seated at two tables of ten, ignoring them completely in her table travels, even coming as close as the table next to theirs, the snooty piece of shit. Didn't she know her husband needed all his personnel in order to be as successful as he was in his business. He couldn't do it all by himself; that's why they were invited to the wedding— screw her!

The men who worked in the field were not invited. There were too many if you counted their wives as well, and since the wives could not be excluded, he decided not to invite them. Nina was glad they weren't there, because the bride certainly would have snubbed them too, and they would have felt the disrespect as did the office staff. The men in the field had to be treated with high regard; their work was to be acknowledged as valuable or they could steal, steal, steal. She had a lot to learn.

Jim danced with Nina, giving her the chance to wish him happiness until his new wife resentfully broke in, knowing how close they were. Nina told her to take good care of him.

Jim remarked at one time that he learned you could love a lot of people in different ways. One is passion and lust, the way he loved so many women.

Friendship leads to love for a man as well as a woman. He loved his superintendent who handled all the field men and the work, making the job easier for him. His respect for Nina and her devotion to him and the company was filled with love.

His wife of eighteen years was comfort, food, and shelter with the strongest love forever because they had children together.

His new wife would be an adventure in his fifties. He did not know how this younger woman would react to his oldie-moldy friends in their later years, when she would still feel she was young and wanted to associate with those her age who didn't have wrinkled skin yet. Who knows?

Chapter Fourteen

Inspiration

Twenty-two years passed before Nina could find the time to go back to her book, back to the time she lived near the dumps in Lily, Indiana. She had made it to the top. She was successful in her work, and her husband was most successful in his, a trucking/excavating company with contracts with two steel mills, South Works in Chicago and Gary Works in Indiana. Their son went on to a great job in sunny California. Eventually they moved there to be near him and his family. One rainy California winter, Nina finished her book. She was the only one alive of her family in the year 1997.

The written pages of her story lay in a dresser drawer for fifty years.

From the time Nina was twelve years old she made notes of the places where they lived and all the happenings, the people and their hardships, the joys and decisions in life during their quest for survival during the Depression years.

So in the year 1958, when her little son was three years old, taking naps daily and no longer needing his mother to watch over him constantly, pull up or down his pants, get him a drink of water, or play with him, Nina turned to reading book after book.

Rickey begged for companionship from the neighborhood children his age, giving his mother much free time. Nina's husband worked very long hours, so she had evening time on her hands as well.

One day she finished reading a book that prompted her to say, "What a disappointment. Why, I'll bet I could write a story better than that."

While Rickey napped, his mother began writing. Her remarkable memory of the past revealed a vivid picture of the most unusual place where once she lived for eleven years and booklike characters that were associated with her family—mostly Russians, their comrades, their poverty, their strife, mixed with contentment to be in America enjoying a freedom like never known before.

Nina began to write swiftly with authenticity; it flowed easily, making it a true saga of long ago. She had hopes of describing the place that once existed where they had lived and to make the characters leap off the pages for readers.

She began remembering that to have been poor then was to enjoy looking at a Sears Roebuck catalog, wishing for that doll or baseball mitt, or to dream of being embraced by your first love.

Having been poor means being rich in appreciation for the rest of your life. The voices were returning of the persons in her story and the scenes of recollection, yet knowing her mother could contribute much to her writing, she began making a list of questions she would ask her to answer.

Nadia was feeling very lonely the day Rickey and

Nina drove to Winsome to see her. They brought her back with them to spend a few days at their home. Nadia's husband, Alex, had been dead for eight years, and her son and daughters lived some distances away.

Nadia lived by choice all alone in the six-room frame house that her husband bought when she came to America to join him after a ten-year separation. She had wondered how her liquor-loving husband could have saved enough money to purchase the house. He gave her no specific answer. She kept questioning him. He would just laugh, not looking at her nor meeting her eyes. He would then get up, leave the room, and go to his hiding place in the basement where he kept his liquor supply to have a drink or two. She kept asking.

One day while sober, he whispered to her that the boarding house he had lived in had four boarders, all Russians, just like he. Each was waiting to make contact with loved ones in the old country. One of these men died suddenly. He had no family, because he did not know where they were or what happened to them during the war and revolution in Russia. This man occupied the room next to Alex. Alex knew he was saving his money to send for his wife and family if they were ever found. He never put his money in a bank; few did in those days.

Alex found four thousand dollars in cash under the deceased man's bed mattress. There was no one to report it to. He kept the money and nervously put a down payment on the house so his family would have a home when they arrived to join him in America, knowing they would soon be on their way. He felt if he had not found the money, someone else would have—it was his fortune. All Nadia did was make the sign of the cross when he told her and say, "Oye, oye, oye."

Nadia was welcome to live with any of her children after her husband died, but she loved the small town of Winsome, her house, her widowed neighbor friends, and the swing on the front porch. None of her daughters or son had a front porch large enough to hold a swing. Nadia spent all her spare time on the swing, even in winter. Many friends walking by, seeing her there, stopped to talk or even to join her on the swing, filling her loneliness and sharing a lifetime of memories.

She would say it was good to be alive even if it was raining, snowing, cold, or hot. Weather did not affect her disposition because she could remember and had endured much more displeasure than the discomfort of weather, such as being hungry, lost, very cold, miles and miles away from home and family not knowing if she would ever see them again, the terror of war that seemed never to end, and the wonderment of will it ever get better?

This was her recollection of her Russia, and it was affirmed by many of the persons who joined her on the swing: Polish, Slovak, Ukrainian, Russian, Lithuanian, and even Jew (Russian Jew), all with the same desire—to have a better life for their children.

Nina and her mother sat at the kitchen table drinking tea, and Nina began questioning her mother about the past. Naturally, she had to tell her mother why she was asking so many questions. Nadia was delighted to hear that Nina was finally going to do the thing she had always wanted to do—write her book.

She answered eagerly and added much to the characters, events, time, and places her daughter was inquiring about. So, she began fashioning her story around their lives, beginning in the old country a long time ago.

Nina's husband knew nothing of what she was doing in her spare time. "I read," was the reply she gave him to his asking. She loved to read. She would read every book she could get her hands on when time would permit.

Her most treasured possession (other than her son, Rickey) was in her bookcase—a green, leather-bound copy of *A Hundred and One Famous Poems*—a present from a dear old friend who took her under his wing and opened the door to the fascinating world of books and their ownership. That the authors could make her, then a girl of sixteen, wish for something that at the time she thought was impossible and highly improbable—to be an author—made her experience the mixed feeling of respect and indignation toward every author of every book she had read after the first.

To the nickname of "Skinny" at the time she added the name "Bookworm." When she was finally able to earn money, she bought her own books. The possession of these writings was much more enjoyable. She did not have to read them hurriedly as she did with library books, and she could read them over again if she could not afford to buy more when her supply was exhausted.

Nina had no special friends. There were few friends to be had in the place where they once lived. Yes, she spoke to her classmates in school and was an

A student, but she retired to her deep thoughts while walking the paths in Lily, and she turned to animism towards the sun, trees, birds, clouds, and stars as she spoke to imaginary souls knowing she needed to put it all into words one day. She had a lot to say.

She bought a lined-paper, leather-bound book she treated as a diary and found great pleasure in writing all her thoughts into it each day. The pages were not large enough for all the words she had within her, so she used scraps of anything she could find to write on.

As she began writing, actual spoken words flashed back into her mind as though some of the dead persons whom she was writing about were before her, encouraging her, telling her what to say. For days she pondered over names, trying to find suitable substitutes, but decided to change only the last names of every person she was writing about. This way, she felt confusion would be avoided, and perhaps later she might make more definite changes.

She had doubts of selling her book for publication and looked upon her scribblings as a hobby to complete one day for the enjoyment of her family and friends and most of all for all who lived in the place once known as Lily, Indiana. Then confidence filled her being, and she began writing until she could no longer keep her eyes open.

When her household chores were done, with great anticipation she quickly returned to the project she had begun. When the first draft was written, not being able to keep her secret, time-consuming work to herself any longer, she told her husband what she had accomplished.

He asked what she was writing about and nothing

more—no objections, comments, suggestions, or interest to read it. Give him a newspaper and he would read it from beginning to end or a magazine filled with pictures of girls with long tresses partially covering their nude breasts and he would look at it from cover to cover. He did not have the time to sit still and read a book; they were too lengthy for him. Even if someone were to tell him it was sexy, he was not interested.

When she was in the middle of putting together her second draft with corrections and additions, she was faced with a choice of continuing or giving it up. Her sisters learned she was writing a book. Presuming she was writing about her family and had information regarding everyone's clandestine affairs, they decided among themselves to inform Nina that they would sue her. Better yet, they wished she would die before she finished her works.

She was shocked into incredulity to learn what transpired during her absence at a New Year's Eve family gathering. She had begun to hope they would encourage her and perhaps even help by adding more remembrances, knowing that she, an unselfish person, would make them benefit from her book if she ever sold it. However, she was mainly writing it for her family and posterity. The thought of money never entered her mind.

Chapter Fifteen

New Year's Eve

"I hope my Nina be rich some day." Nadia absent-mindedly, softly, spoke in her broken English as she sat in a chair while Butter, her youngest daughter, was setting her hair.

Vera, her eldest daughter, born in Russia, heard her and asked, "What did you say?"

"Oh, nothing," Nadia replied, wishing she had not said what she did. She thought no one heard her.

"I heard you," Butter added as she stopped combing her mother's hair.

It was a New Year's Eve gathering at Butter's house. Nadia was spending the long weekend with her youngest daughter and family. Vera and Daria (another daughter) were there with their husbands. Nina and her husband could not make it. The streets were sheets of glass. It had rained, then turned very cold, then it snowed and more rain fell that day, then zero temperatures, making the roads hazardous. Nina lived ten miles away from Butter, and they thought it best not to travel that night.

"Come on, tell us what you meant by that," Vera insisted. "Why do you want Nina to get rich? Why not Butter, Daria, or me? And how about your only son? Sonny needs money more than any of us—he has four little kids." She was waiting for her mother to answer.

Butter butted in with, "Yeah, Ma, come on, tell us why you want her to be rich?"

Nadia laughed, then answered with Russian idioms, "I want all my kids to be rich. I no mean only Nina."

"She doesn't need any money. She has everything she needs. Or is something wrong with Nina that she needs money?" questioned Butter.

"No, no," Nadia replied, shaking her head. "I sorry I said that. I was thinking it be nice if one my girls be very rich some day."

Butter returned to twisting and pinning her mother's just-washed hair and asked, "Well, how can Nina do that?"

"I dunno," Nadia said with a smile on her face. She could never hold a straight face whenever she was not telling the truth, and neither could any of her children.

Suddenly Vera sat upright, clapped her hands together and declared, "I'll betcha I know. She must be writing her book."

Nadia laughed but said nothing.

Butter stopped what she was doing and stepped in front of her mother. Removing the bobby pins from her mouth, she looked into Nadia's upturned face and asked, "Is she, Ma?"

Daria came out of the kitchen holding a cigarette in one hand and a tall glass of beer in the other.

The three husbands were in the kitchen, sitting at

the table, talking about the plans for the large play-
room Butter's husband, Scott, was going to add on to
the back end of his house that coming spring.

Daria sat down beside Vera on the couch. "What's
going on?" she inquired.

"Mama has a secret and she won't tell us," Vera
answered. "She slipped and said she thinks Nina will
be rich some day."

"No, I no sayit that," Nadia corrected.

"That's what you meant," Butter said, shaking the
comb in front of her mother's face.

Vera said, "Yes, yes, I'll bet I guessed it. Look at her
guilty face," as she pointed at her mother.

Nadia laughed again. She felt as though she was on
the witness stand with her daughters as the prosecu-
tors, shaking their fingers at her, insisting that she con-
fess to the truth.

Vera went on, "We all know Nina wanted to write
one day. That's the only way I can figure out that she
would be rich."

Daria took a puff on her cigarette and then asked,
"Why would she want to keep it a secret?"

Nadia answered this: "She no wanit you to make
fun of her."

"Ah ha!" exclaimed Butter. "Then she is writing a
book."

"Yes," affirmed Nadia.

"See there, I guessed it," Vera said as she folded her
arms and leaned back against the couch. "I knew it the
day she asked me a couple of questions about Russia.
Nina was over at my house with Mama a few weeks
ago, and the two of them started talking about Russia.
Mama was even crying remembering the past. I didn't

say anything then, but I had the thought that Nina was gathering information. We talked about the four years of World War I from the time the Bolshevik Revolution was going on in Russia until it all ended in 1919 and how we traveled in cattle cars to Siberia and slept in igloos. Many people didn't even have shoes, just rags on top of rags wrapped round and round. We looked in garbage cans for scraps of food. We ate potato peelings. Bread was like gold. Soup was water, weeds, and bones—potatoes when we could find them. I was young, but I remember."

Vera stopped shortly and sighed deeply, then continued: "We saw so much death that we looked at them as sleeping people; no one had time to check. It was so cold we wanted to just curl up and die. Mama and I said we would never talk about the past. Oh hell, I don't want to remember all that." Vera suddenly stopped talking.

Butter went back to fixing her mother's hair again. Daria puffed on her cigarette and sipped her beer. This was the first time they heard Vera say so much about her life in Russia. They did not ask her. They really did not want to know—it was too sad.

Nadia wished to spare her children the horror stories of war, so she talked about it only when she was asked, and then she did not elaborate. It was easier on the heart to forget than to remember.

Nadia spoke: "Yes, I think it nice Nina findit time to do what she always wanit do. Olga (Butter) is happy; she is mother now. Sonny haveit four nice kids an good job. An Daria go to California like she always wanit. An Vera haveit easy life now. An now my Nina turn. I wanit all my kids be happy an doit what they dream to do in life."

Daria snuffed out her cigarette in the large black ashtray on the table beside her and wondered out loud, "What the hell could she be writing about?"

"Yeah, I wonder," pondered Butter, looking perplexed.

Vera reported seriously, "A person writes best about the things they know. She must be writing about us—what else?"

Immediately Daria responded matter-of-factly, "She better not," as she crossed her legs and pulled her skirt down as far as it would go over her knees.

Whispering and smiling, Butter questioned, "Why? Ya got something to hide?"

"Sure, plenty," replied Daria with a grin.

Still whispering, Butter asked, "What? What?"

In reply, Daria snickered with a smile, "Wouldn't you like to know."

"Hmmm. I have a secret too. My husband would leave me if he found out," Butter related. She was finished curling her mother's hair. She placed the box of pins and comb on the cocktail table and sat down beside Vera on the couch.

Vera quietly said, "Mine would leave me too if he found out about me."

"And so would mine," Daria admitted to her sisters.

Butter ascertained, "Hmmm, this is true confessions night."

Nadia returned the straightback chair that was being used while Butter was fixing her hair to the kitchen, then came back into the living room. She sat down in Scott's favorite leather chair and stretched her legs out on the ottoman.

Butter lit a cigarette. "Well, do we tell or do we keep our secrets?" she queried. Not waiting for answers, she said, "I'll bet we could all write a book."

Daria theorized, "Well, Nina doesn't know anything about my secrets, so she can't be writing about me."

Butter's turn: "That leaves me out too. How about you Vera?"

Reflectively, Vera finally said, "I was just thinking. Mama knows my secrets, and she's been spending a lot of time at Nina's house. Did you tell her anything?" She looked at her mother searchingly.

"I tellit her everything she want to know," answered Nadia.

"Oh, you did!" Vera said in surprise. "About me? What did you tell her?"

"No, I no tellit her nothing 'bout you, only 'bout Lily an Russia," informed Nadia.

Vera's tone of voice revealed her anger. "Oh, about Russia. I suppose you told her about the time I was captured by German soldiers during the war?"

"What?" Daria asked in surprise.

"You were?" Butter asked. She was just as surprised as Daria.

Vera laughed, "Yes, I was. But I won't tell you any more than that." She glanced first at Daria, then at Butter, and then looked at her mother. "If you told Nina what happened to me and she writes it in her book, Mama . . . Did you?"

"No," Nadia replied. "Nina askit nothing 'bout

you. You was little girl then. Soldiers gave you food. Lucky I find you an we run away."

Vera responded, "Yes, but people will read between the lines, and she could make up something that people might believe."

"Oh, Vera, don't get all upset. Mama said she didn't tell Nina about you, so what are you worried about? Sure, people read between the lines—let 'um. There's nothing you could do about that," Butter offered.

Vera countered loudly, "Oh, yes I can. I'll stop her. I'll kill her if she's writing about me. Who does she think she is that she could ruin my life?"

"Vera!" Butter snapped. She pointed towards the kitchen. "They'll hear us."

Vera lowered her eyes and nervously began twisting her shoulder-length hair.

Daria offered, "Maybe she's writing about Mama?"

In answer Nadia said, "So what if she writeit 'bout me? I no care. Let her. She writeit true story."

"Oh, Mama, how could you sit there and say you don't care? People are funny. They believe things that are written even if you say they aren't true," Vera proffered.

"So what? No let people bother you. They no putit food on you table. When Nina sellit her book we all be rich, you knowit that," returned Nadia.

"Who wants money? I'd rather have a good name," Vera admonished.

"You gotit good name. All my kids good—everybody knowit that," stated Nadia.

"Still, if she writes about you or any of us and I can prove it, I'll sue her," declared Vera.

Nadia laughed and said, "No, you silly."

"Yeah, we'll see," Vera rebuked.

Nadia reasoned, "Yes, we will see when she finish book."

"We'll all sue her, Ma," notified Daria, who was still ashamed of where her family lived at one time and did not want her secret revealed to her friends, whom she told she had no family, that she lived with an aunt—a big lie.

"We sure will sue her," Butter agreed. "Nobody's going to write about my mother." She was reflecting on the past, remembering how pretty her mother was and how many men liked her, wondering if she told Nina things she should not know and might write about that could hurt her mother.

"Who's writing about your mother?" Scott asked as he entered the living room and heard the ending of his wife's sentence. The other two brothers-in-law followed him into the living room. None of the men sat down. They stood and stretched their bodies after having sat so long at the kitchen table.

Butter replied to Scott's question, "Nina's writing a book."

Scott released a loud guffaw. His brothers-in-law joined him in laughter. Everyone joined in. Scott slapped his thigh and said, "That's the best one I've heard in a long time!"

Vera laughed so hard that tears came to her eyes. This was a habit over which she had no control. When she stopped laughing, she wiped her eyes and said, "It won't be so funny when she writes all our family secrets."

"What secrets?" the husbands asked in unison as the laughter ceased among them.

Butter attempted to sound mysterious when she said, "Don't you know every family has skeletons in their closets? Nina's going to bring them out in her book, and they're gonna haunt us."

"As long as they don't have little hatchets and chop us up," Scott responded. "Let her write. More power to her. I hope she writes about all of us, then we'll sue 'er and get all her money."

"We already decided that," Butter announced as she stood up and asked, "Coffee, anyone?"

The men said they wanted beer. The ladies went into the kitchen to have coffee and to talk further about what they were going to do now that they knew their sister was writing a book. They were worried she was going to expose facts they thought she could not know unless her mother told her, unless she was a wizard and could read their minds. She would uproot their past that was now coming back swiftly before them with guilt.

Chapter Sixteen

The Visit

The following week, after a break in the weather allowed travel on the roadways with less danger, Vera decided to go and see Nina. She took her mother along. Immediately upon entering her back door and removing their boots that were snow coated, Vera said, "We came to find out what you are writing about in your book." They removed their coats and sat next to each other at the kitchen table.

Taking a chair across from them, Nina asked, "How do you know I'm writing a book?" Looking at her mother, she stated, "You promised you wouldn't tell anybody."

Vera answered, "She didn't tell us. I guessed it."

"Us? Who's us?" Nina wanted to know.

"All of your sisters," Vera informed her. "We all want to know what you are writing about."

The unexpected interrogation prompted Nina to say, "I'd rather not tell you. It will spoil everything. It's just about people."

"What people? Are you writing about your family?"

"I said I'd rather not say. Can't you wait until I finish it?"

Vera pounded her fist on the table, exclaiming, "No, I can't! I have to know now!"

"What is this? Why are you so worried about what I'm writing? What is the matter with you?"

"I'll tell you what's the matter. We know Mama has been spending a lot of time here, and she knows a lot of our secrets. We used to tell her everything. We think she told you everything about us."

Nina shook her head and said, "No, Vera, she didn't. I don't know everybody's secrets. Mama could tell you the things I asked her about."

Nadia spoke: "I tellit her but she no believe me."

Looking at Vera, Nina responded, "You don't believe your own mother? What do you want to believe?"

Pounding the table once more, Vera replied, "I want to believe that you won't write anything bad about my family. You know a book with sex in it will sell good. Your book must have sex in it or you wouldn't be writing, because you wouldn't be able to sell it. Mama probably told you lots of things about her daughters that nobody should know. If you write about us, we'll sue you. I mean it! We will sue you!"

Nina laughed, "Why, you have everything figured out, don't you? I see the whole problem now. You think I know how many men my sisters slept with and that's all I'm writing about, just to make my book sell. Well, you are wrong. I know nothing like that about my sisters."

Angrily, Vera declared, "But people will read between the lines."

In rebuttal Nina asked, "Well, what am I supposed to do about that?"

"There is something I can do about it. How would you like it if you were the cause for your sisters' marriages breaking up? Daria and Butter have secrets their husbands don't know about and maybe you do. If you write them in your book and they read it, they'll leave them. I suppose you wouldn't care, just as long as your book made money?"

Nina exclaimed, "That's not true! In the first place, I won't be breaking up marriages. I don't know my sisters' secrets. How could I? Mama didn't tell me, and sisters don't tell sisters how many men they said yes to. I'm supposing this is the only thing that a woman keeps secret, and I don't think a husband who really loves his wife is going to leave her because of her wrongdoings before he married her. The past is dead. Let it lie. In the second place, if they believe everything I'm going to write, then they are wrong again. And, in the third place, I might not even sell my book. You have all just jumped to conclusions due to your own guilt, and all these accusations have no basis whatsoever. You must have something you want awfully bad to hide or you wouldn't even be here now."

Admittedly, Vera said, "Yes, I do. Mama must have told you what happened to me in Russia, and you must be writing about it and making it worse than it was just to sell your story."

Nadia stepped in, saying, "No, no, Vera, you wrong."

Vera turned to her mother and loudly said, "Don't tell me you didn't tell her about the soldiers that captured me in Russia? Did you tell her I was pregnant before I got married? I don't want my kids to know."

"Vera," Nina interrupted and shouted, "stop right there. Don't reveal any of your past to me, because I don't want to hear it. This is the first I'm hearing about soldiers capturing you. Mama told me nothing about this, believe me. And so what if you were pregnant—at least you got married. This is ridiculous."

Vera pounded the table and said, "Then prove it to me that you are not writing about me or your mother or any of your sisters. Prove it! Let me see what you have written!"

Calmly, Nina talked, knowing that further shouting would waken her son. She said, "You have to take my word for it. I can't show you what I have written. I could, but I won't. I am so disappointed in all of you that you could think such terrible things. You will just have to wait until I'm done and maybe I'll let you read it."

"Then why did you keep it a secret? You must be hiding something," Vera questioned and expected an answer.

"Only the sentimental thoughts I have had all my life of my youth. You know I always wanted to write some day. I never had the time until now, but you are making it something ugly by all your insinuations. What do you want me to do, quit?"

"Yes, that's just what I want you to do," resolved Vera with her eyes wide open and lips pursed.

"No, no. Nina, no listen to her," Nadia chimed in. "She only jealous she no write it book she self."

Vera differed, "No, Mama, I don't want to write a book. I don't need the money that bad. I'll think of my family first before I think of money."

It was Nina's turn to defend herself. "There you go

again, thinking I am writing bad things about my family. Can't I make you believe that I am writing about people—all kinds of people?"

"No, you can't. An author writes best about people she knows, and we are the people you know. I know you have sex in it, and people will point their fingers at us. That's how people are. Why don't you prove it to me that I'm wrong? Show it to me."

"You know I can't do that. What's to stop you from keeping it and copying it? And, what's to stop me from changing it after you leave? If you don't have enough trust in me then I don't owe you anything. I'm sorry you don't believe me and can't understand how books are written, but there is nothing I can do about it. You will just have to wait until I'm done. Maybe I'll never finish it. Maybe I'll never sell it."

"Well I'm going to make sure you don't. I'm going to tear it up." With that Vera got up from her chair and went into the living room. Not finding what she was looking for, she went into the bedrooms and glanced around, looking for paperwork. She woke Rickey when she opened his bedroom door. He came out of his room and ran to his mother.

Nina hugged her son and kissed him. She did not move to put a stop to Vera's wanderings throughout the house, knowing her writing was in a safe place—in the refrigerator. She and Rickey went to the grocery store that morning, and Nina could think of no better fireproof hiding place for her draft.

Nadia left her chair and went to Vera. She said, "Vera, you makeit only trouble for youself. Come, we go home." She took hold of her daughter's hand.

Vera wrenched herself free and said, "She can't write this book, Ma. She's gonna hurt all of us."

"Where is it?" she asked Nina when she returned to the kitchen. "Why are you hiding it? Now I know what kind of girl you are. How could you think so much of money?"

Rickey spoke, "Don't holler. You're bad for hollering."

Nina said, "Vera, will you please leave my house."

She answered, "Yes, I will leave your house, but not until you promise you won't write your book."

Shaking her head, Nina told her, "No. I want to write it even more now just to prove to you how ridiculous you have all been."

"We will see about that—we'll see."

"In about a year or two, Vera. It will be a long wait."

"I'll be the first to buy it when it comes out."

"But what if I don't get it published—then what? Do you think I should let my sisters read it? After this, maybe I shouldn't, and maybe I won't."

"Oh, don't worry, you will sell it if it has sex in it, but you won't see me or any of your sisters in your house again. Go ahead and write your book. You will see us all in court! But, I hope you drop dead before you finish it." Vera picked up her coat and went to the door to put on her boots. Her face was flushed from anger, not having achieved what she set out to do—destroy Nina's writings.

Nadia kissed Nina and Rickey good-bye and reached for her coat.

"Stay here and play with me, Gramma," Rickey offered.

"No, honey, I can't," Nadia refused. "I have to go home with Vera. I come pretty soon an play with you all day."

Nina said to her mother, "I wish you would stay."

"No, I go home with Vera. I sorry I tell them you writeit book. If I know Vera makeit trouble like this, I not come here today."

"Aren't they silly, Mama? They don't even know what I'm writing about. I'll never tell them."

"Yes, they silly. They jealous they not writeit book."

"Well, give them time. They will realize how foolish they have been."

"I know. No listen to them. I hope I live to see your book."

Nadia left the house to join Vera in the car. Rickey ran to the living room window to wave to them. He returned to the kitchen and announced, "Mom, they didn't wave to me."

Nina replied, "Well, maybe they will next time."

"What should I do?" she asked her husband the evening of the day the big scene between her and her older sister Vera took place. "Should I give it up?"

He answered, "What are you worried about? I wouldn't let any of them bother me. Don't let them stop you from doing something you always wanted to do."

"When they left I was more determined than ever to finish just to show them how wrong they are. I know nothing of what they are accusing me of. I am writing a true story. If they don't like it, then so be it."

"That's just what I would do," he said as he picked up the newspaper and began reading the front page, which to her meant the conversation was ended. He wanted no interruptions while he read the paper. Even Rickey knew he was not to bother his father when he read. A cigarette in his hand also meant Rickey could not climb on his father's lap until the cigarette was put out. Nina was highly in favor of the latter, but not the former. He saw very little of his son, but Nina really did not mind his long absences now; she was too busy writing.

She went on writing to completion, placed her work in a box in a dresser drawer, and did not look at her manuscript until fifty years later, after her entire family was deceased. Nina could not fathom the loss of her family, the only family she had, who so vehemently objected to her writings. It was not worth it to her—they meant more to her than her book.

Chapter Seventeen

Epilogue

This is the continued story of the characters in that book. This is Nina's answer to readers of her book who wondered, "What happened to everybody?"

NADIA

Nadia lived to the age of seventy-two, enjoying the upbringing of Sonny, her treasured only son who looked so much like his father, Alex, until her tired Russian heart stopped. In her repose, her fingernails were manicured for the first time, and the wedding band she found on the dumps was still on her finger.

Her entire life was dedicated to her children. She wanted the very best for them; if they were happy, she was happy. Her family would never forget how she became so accustomed to living alone that when it came time for meals, she never set a table or took a dish out of her cabinets—she ate right out of the pot while standing at the stove. Her girls would scold her, but to no avail; she would just laugh and say, "It habit." Should they bring her a present, she would ask them to take it back and not spend their money on her, saying, "I not need it." She was a Russian woman with a heart of gold.

One of the traditions from the old country was to wear a *babushka*, even in the house, just like Matka Boska (Madonna, mother of Christ) did. She always had her head covered, and Nadia revered this tradition, as did all Russian women. Nadia's braid of honey blonde hair that she had cut off as her daughter Vera insisted, to have her in the style of that period, is in Nina's possession to this day.

She was also very superstitious, which led her to believe that if you left home, forgot to take money, and went back to get it, you should not go on your journey and should stay home. It meant bad luck, that something bad would happen to you.

Another superstition was: if there is a thread to be cut off the cloth you are wearing, you must place a piece of the garment in your mouth before cutting off the piece of thread—or else bad luck.

Bird droppings on your person or nearby meant death to someone you know or are close to.

She also read cards as gypsies do, as she learned in Russia. If someone told her a dream, she had a meaning for the dreamer—bad mixed with good.

Many times she reminisced about the love of Stephan, her Polish love, and was much saddened that he ended his life when she left him. It was a love of passion, friendship, and comfort after the horror of war experienced by her daughter Vera and herself when she was still a young woman who felt there was no hope of ever going to America to join her husband after ten long years of separation. Adding to this past sorrow, many times she was reminded of the hardships in Lily,

Indiana, and made the sign of the cross in gratitude to God for her children having survived living there.

Nadia had repeatedly warned her daughters never to go inside Indian Joe's house.

A number of times Nina was asked by Crazy Catherine, his housekeeper, to go to the Costello's and fetch a half pint of whiskey and earn a nickel for the errand; however, she was never to accept the invitation of entering his house. God bless that her girls honored their mother's advice, however, fifteen-year-old Helen often entered his house while delivering whiskey and the newspaper. This led to him impregnating the very young errand girl who was paid with nickels and dimes.

Her most sad memory of her husband, Alex, was when she took a half pint of whiskey from his pocket while he stood on the porch, hands on his hips, and swore, "*Yebitvou mat* (fuck your mother—in Russian)," then added, "Son of a bitch, son of a bitch!"

She ran with it to the well and poured half its contents into another bottle that lay beside the well (bottles were kept there for water that Alex carried in his pocket when he went to cut hay in the fields with his sickle).

She then added water to it and mixed some sand into it. The other half pint she buried in the dirt by the well and said out loud, "I do it again next time when he get drunk an no go to work."

He was still standing on the porch when she returned, handed him the bottle with the sand in it, and said, "Awright, here you whiskey. Go ahead an die, I no care."

"*Te Kurva, Te Kurva!*" he swore, calling her a whore.

Alex grabbed the bottle from her outstretched hand and went into his shed. He did not come out until the next day. He had a cot in there to sleep on. He hid the whiskey in a barrel of chicken feed and went to sleep.

The next day he paid ten cents for a dog that was kept in the shed at all times as the protector of his hidden whiskey habit that he enjoyed so much.

Nadia agonized, knowing his precious drink was filled with sand and water and that he drank it anyway. She wished her husband did not drink, knowing it would eventually kill him.

The things we say and do oftentimes come back to haunt us, as this did to her for many years.

Another melancholy remembrance was of all the turkeys she tried to raise every year with no success; they lived to weigh only two pounds and then died. She knew of no one to ask how to make them survive and grow, yet she tried year after year.

Ducks, geese, chickens, pigs, the goat, and her cow were routine and easy to nourish and have prosper to maturity until time to adorn the family dinner table.

Nadia's secret was having given birth to a girl child when in Russia, fathered by her Polish lover. She brought her to America, where she was accepted as a niece with love and gratitude by all.

Now Nadia wanted her daughter to write about everything, feeling as elder persons do in their late years: What is there to hide? That's life. This or that does not make you bad. Everyone is in search of love; it is the greatest sustenance to carry on.

Even the exchange of partners in the Costello hayloft was good people enjoying a diversion from life's drudgery of work, work, work. Yes, liquor consumption contributed to their behavior, but they took it lightly, knowing they were all friends and would remain friends.

In those days they did not even have a radio in their homes because there was no electricity. There was no escape or contact with the outside world, and no relatives to come visit—they were still in Russia. Fun in the hayloft was just fun in the hayloft. One time Nina saw her mother and Alex in the exchange, but she did not write it in her book. She tried to understand, yet she was ashamed to witness this sin.

BUTTER

Butter, the youngest daughter, had a heart attack and died in her husband's arms when she was fifty-eight. They had two children, goldfish, and a summer cottage on a lake in Michigan that reminded her of Lily Pad Lake where she romped as a child, her most joyous years.

She enjoyed the sweets that she was deprived of in her youth, always remembering not having a penny to spend when stopping at Lily Store. She went just to look at all the gum balls, peanuts, sugared watermelon slices, Tootsie Rolls, bull's eyes, chocolate-covered raisins, Hershey's bars, peanut-butter- and caramel-filled chocolates, licorice sticks, malteds, suckers, jelly beans, fudge, bubble gum, and—best of all—Tootsie Pops, because they lasted the longest.

To find a penny on the ground was like finding gold to the youngsters in those days. They couldn't run fast enough to the store, then took a long time to choose a treat, making Albert, the storekeeper, make many trips back and forth to ask if they had made up their mind.

The Fourth of July holiday was a most exciting time. It meant they saw a parade and were given money for ice cream at the park. But the day after was much more exciting, when they would all go to the park looking for coins on the ground that were carelessly dropped by the many picnickers and revelers, much to the gain of Sonny, Butter, their friend Nanny who was always with them, and Nina, the leader of the gang, the runner who ran all the time, the young lady who always planned to write about all the fun they had had in those days.

Sure enough, they always found coins in the park before the park cleanup workers did because they went there early in the morning. Finding a dime would last them all week and more. Knowing it would be a long time before they had money again for sweet treats at Lily Store, they would only purchase one or two pieces at a time.

It was even more fun to just go and look at everything behind the glass cases and wonder which one to buy next time. If they found a quarter, they were so overjoyed that the thought of spending it did not come easy; they seldom saw a coin so large. They fingered it, rolled it around, tossed it up in the air to catch it—heaven forbid if it ever fell on the ground and could not be found or if someone else grabbed it and ran off. It was spent only as a last resort. If they found one, someone would sleep with it clutched in his or her hand and wake with a sweaty palm from holding it so tightly.

At seventeen, Butter was a mother. She loved dolls

when she was young, dreamed of owning a store-bought one, but she cherished her picaninny doll (as she named it) with braids all over her head that her mother found on the dumps and had only one doll with blonde hair and a pretty pink party dress and white shoes and socks—she can't remember how she got it.

Her daughter, Nancy, looked exactly like Butter, with blonde curly hair, blue-green eyes, and a full face. She was not interested in playing with dolls. Nancy wore guns and a holster, cowboy hat, boots, and a neckerchief just like her brother, Bobby. She even walked the way cowboys walk, with her thumbs tucked into her pants at her waist and taking long strides.

She refused to wear dresses, not even party dresses—especially party dresses.

They did not go to church or any special place too often, so her mother did not attempt to dress Nancy like a girl.

As for pets, Butter always said she would have many; they had none. Nancy was asthmatic, which prohibited any type of pet in the house.

Nancy was allergic to her own hair, so it had to be tied back as far away from her face as possible. She was violently allergic to house dust, so her mother was forever cleaning house.

Nevertheless, Butter was content and asked no more from life than what she had. She loved life, laughed a lot, and worried about nothing. Her smile was like butter to the end.

If anyone wanted to be cheered, all he or she had to do was call Butter; she was full of anecdotes to make them laugh and feel lighthearted. Knowing what a stressful job her sister (favorite sister) had, she sent Nina a card that had nothing on it except these words in bold letters: **AW, FUCK IT!** Guaranteed to make anyone smile.

Butter's secret was that at the age of twelve, she and Nanny, the boy next door and constant playmate, pulled their pants down one day when they were underneath their favorite tree that held their swing and experimented with their young bodies. Her brother, Sonny, watched, laughed, and finally said they were silly; he left them to go and catch frogs.

She felt Nina always knew because Nina knew everything, but she did not write this in her first book, nor that Butter also experimented with her young brother who shared the same bed with her each night until Nina caught them and shamed them and told them the facts of fife.

Sex awareness comes at an early age. It was no big deal.

SONNY

Sonny (Peter), the only son, was blond and blue-eyed like his father. The favorite, he graduated high school with sports honors and accepted a contract to play farm team baseball with the New York Yankees for one year. The second year, Johnny Mostil signed him up with the Chicago White Sox.

Disappointment consumed him. Professional sports permitted swearing, drinking, smoking, and cavorting, totally the opposite of school sportsmanship. He was accustomed to a clean life; the pros were in it for the money.

The army drafted him and sent him to Alaska, where he was stationed for two years. He married his high school cheerleader sweetheart, had four children, divorced, and followed his genetic Russian love for alcohol just like his father, Alex.

However, Sonny was hesitant to get drunk during workdays; he saved this bad habit for weekends only. The company he worked for sent him to school for six years to become a specialized instrument man in its gasoline refinery, a most tedious, momentous occupation that demanded sobriety.

He was devastated by the divorce that left him with no family to go home to, so he lived in an apartment in Winsome near a tavern on the corner that supplied him with conversation from its many patrons such as himself—the barstool crowd, lonely people in need of laughter and companionship.

He never married again. He loved his first wife like he could love no other.

After open-heart bypass surgery he continued drinking, and of course smoking, and died at the age of sixty-two—their beloved Sonny—light of their lives— the kid who loved his dog, Buster, loved his sisters, mother and father.

His sisters, Nina and Butter, were so close to him all their young lives that they would always remember him with a stick in his hand as he ran, jumped, climbed, swam, and partook in his most favorite summertime sport of catching frogs (bugeyes, as he called them). He would catch them with his bare hands and carry them home in his pockets, much to the astonishment of his family. His companions used a net, if they brought one at the time, or a rag, bag, or just used leaves to cover their hands from the slimy critters who tasted so good when fried in butter and salt.

When he set the barns on fire accidentally, he was forgiven instantly because he was so loved and did not perish in his hiding place in the house. The girls were responsible for his safety; after all, Alex waited twenty years before having a son.

Sonny was devoted to his father and inherited the agility and coordination that enabled him to excel in all sports, even football. He was shorter than any player on the team, so when Nina and her mother went to the games, they saw Sonny make many a touchdown due to his running ability after catching the ball. The crowd would yell his name repeatedly in its mania for him to go into the game, but the coach would permit him only to catch and run, not wanting his star player to get hurt.

His name and photo often filled the sports pages of the newspapers. He was well liked by all that knew him. He never had a confrontation with anyone. A smile perpetuated his face—that's how happy he was all the time.

He missed being with his children after the divorce, but he saw them as often as they were available.

At his wake, Nina remembered that he went to four different fast-food places for his children because each liked a different kind of hamburger. Now, how many fathers would do that?

And she also remembered and wondered, how many brothers would go to the drug store in town to buy Kotex for his sisters when there was a possibility of being seen by his buddies?

By God! Sonny was special.

In school he was called "Ace," but at home he was

the sweet kid who kissed everyone good-bye before leaving the house, even his father.

He was the fearless little kid who whistled as he passed the lovers in their cars on Lover's Lane. He learned to swim at the age of two with the guidance of his sisters who adored him.

He was the only one that was not afraid of the goat that was named Nanny and later had its name changed to Billy. He would jump on its back and ride it until the goat tired—Sonny did not tire easily.

VERA

Vera had a long life to the age of eighty-one, three children, and a second husband (Frank, her first husband, died of lupus). She worked hard each day to attain cleanliness, as she was brought up in Russia to do, and had few materialistic possessions, as was her communist rearing. She did, however, buy herself a Persian lamb fur coat to keep her warm in winter that reminded her of the cold in Russia—the very, very, cold in Russia—Siberian cold. She often said, "Oh, if only I had a coat like this then."

Her mother, Nadia, bought a fur coat also, only hers had a fur hat to match. When she looked in the mirror wearing her newly acquired raiment she declared, "Now I look like rich Russian *baba* (lady)."

Max Pinkstad, her second husband, a nice country boy in his forties when he married Vera, enjoyed her good soups that she made because when he was young and on the farm they had soup every day. The family called him "Pinky" and her children called him "Dad." They had a long, happy life together. He worked and she tended to the house and all its chores, even cutting the grass and shoveling snow. Pinky let her do these things because she felt she could do it better and to avoid an argument. Being the sweet, quiet, unassuming kind of guy he was, he would just walk away.

Vera's children lived in close proximity to her house yet saw little of her because she was always cleaning, washing, painting, and keeping things immaculate, probably due to how little she had when in Russia. She now treasured what she had and wanted all things to last forever.

Her windows sparkled when the sun shone on them just like when she was in Omsk, Siberia, where they had patrols of men making certain all windows were kept clean. When her family asked her why she worked so hard, her reply was, "Because I am Russian. I am supposed to work hard."

A map of Russia would show that when she and her mother were fleeing the Germans during World War I and for two months traveled in cattle cars from White Russia that was the front lines to Omsk, Siberia, the distance was greater than the whole of the United States of America. The hunger and cold were unimaginable.

Then once again they traveled back the same distance to the shipping ports in hopes of boarding a vessel to America, only to find the ports closed; the war was still on. Selling their ship boarding passes, they traveled a great distance again to find work.

After they made contact with her father, he sent another ship passage that finally brought them to him, and their travels were over. Vera never forgot when as a little girl, skipping rope, she said, "Ha, ha, ha, I'm going to America." She never gave up. Her dream came true at the age of twelve.

Not once did Vera mention Nina's book after the threatening visit fifty years before demanding that she discontinue her writing, not even two days before she died, when Nina called to see how she was feeling. Knowing she did not have long to live, Vera asked her sister if she could spare one thousand dollars to send to her youngest daughter who needed money to buy a car or she couldn't get to work. Communism prompted Vera to ask her sister to share, and Nina did what was asked; she too was a Russian with a big heart.

Before Vera married Max, she had five abortions due to pregnancies with a married man who was great in bed (she could not resist him and therefore got into trouble so many times). Of course she went to her mother to ask what she should do. She already had three children, her husband, Frank, was gone, and she could not have a married man's child.

Her mother offered this solution: In Russia abortions were commonplace; midwives were everywhere, even in the fields. Russians were so poor that they could not afford to have many children. Neither condoms nor birth control even existed, so they used the only method available to them. Otherwise they would have children that would starve to death or die of sickness due to no vaccines, cures, or medicines—and besides, where would they get so many shoes?

Vera took Nadia's advice each time and thought this would be in Nina's book, knowing her mother knew and told the author. This was Vera's secret that prompted her to make an attempt to find and destroy her sister's book, but Nina did not write this in her book . . . it was no big deal.

RICHARD

Did Nina fulfill her dream of Richard and a happy life? Richard—her first love since high school, her dream prince. Yes, they hit it off all right. He liked her and she liked him, but they never became friends, a most important determinant in a relationship. He didn't talk much. He didn't offer any of his thoughts or experiences while in the service during World War II, nor did he even mention school days.

She was most anxious to know whom he took to the school prom, but she did not ask because he did not ask her any questions. Nina was perplexed. She made an attempt to make conversation, but he did not respond.

Dilemma overpowered her, so she remained quiet also. She would see him looking at her as though he was in disbelief to be with her after so much time lapsed since their school days. Or was it that his mind was on others that he would rather be with? Nina would never know.

They had a total of four dates: two movies, one parked car date, and one dancing date at Danceland. They were strangers, young and shy, making going to the movies an easy date. Then it was, "Did you like the movie?" a few comments between them, and then, "Good night, I'll call you." She thanked him and said she had a good time, knowing that's what a girl is supposed to say.

The borrowed car date went really bad. He must have been smitten with her to go to these measures and park in a very dark place near his home. Immediately he began kissing her. She was stunned and began thinking, "What is this? I don't even know him. We are strangers. I can't even see who I'm kissing."

She wished they had gone to the drug store for ice cream instead and talked to get to know one another.

Then suddenly she put her arms around his neck and responded to his amorous advance, remembering this was the young man she dreamed of for years and he was right here at long last.

Unexpectedly, he broke the hold, sat back, and asked, "Where did you learn to kiss like that?"

Once again she was stunned, knew not what to say, then replied, "In the movies."

He made her feel ashamed that she reciprocated, and then she wondered if he thought she was a loose girl.

The truth was that kissing him was easy and natural to her. She loved being loved, loved loving him, but could not say it, remembering when in the school library he sent a note that read: "Why do you stare at me?" She wished she could have responded by saying, "Because I like what I see," but could not do it. Both times she believed should she have answered truthfully, he would have no respect for her, because in those days a man made the first move, not the woman. Should she have exposed her feelings, they would have implied she was after him.

Richard turned the key in the ignition and announced, "Well, this was a mistake." He took her home, neither saying a word all the way.

The dance date was awful. A week after the parking date, with no word from Richard, thinking she would never see him again, she remembered that every Tuesday, Danceland scheduled ladies' night, which meant that a lady could ask a man for a date and dance. She called him and asked if he would like to attend. He accepted and said he would see her at 7:00 P.M.

He was just home from the service, having served in air force communications. He kept looking at old school friends attending the dance and was most anxious to talk to them.

They didn't even dance well together because she was nervous and so was he after the parked car date failure. He was looking around, seeking more friends that might be there, not paying attention to his partner nor even speaking to her.

What was he thinking? Why didn't he say anything? He never even said she looked nice, as a date is supposed to say. What was wrong with him?

She was wondering if he thought of her as a kid who lived on the dumps and was not worthy of being his date, but that was long ago. She knew she had come a long way and yearned to get to know this young man she chose to love in her dreams.

He took her home at ten o'clock. They walked. It was only four blocks away. She could not stay out late; she had to work the next day. They sat on the front porch swing for a short time, but even then no words were exchanged. His mind was elsewhere, and Nina simply could not reach him.

He finally said, "I have nothing to offer you. I'm going away to school. Good-bye." He got up and walked away. She had the feeling he went back to the dance.

The following Saturday Nina accepted a date with a friend who took her to Danceland. Richard was there with another girl. They exchanged hellos when they saw one another, then she began trembling until she thought she would be sick. Her date took her home. The door had closed on her dream. Painful tears wet her pillow many a night, and her thoughts of him never ceased to this day.

In Memoriam

> *My pillow knows that I loved thee,*
> *The quiet one who walked into my heart.*
> *Shy, not speaking, tender young man*
> *Whom I cherished from afar.*
> *Strangers we to the end in farewell*
> *Left tears to wonder until the end of my years,*
> *Should we have been friends first and loved last,*
> *Could we have shared the same pillow?*
> *My dear prince, till the end of time,*
> *Remember me, as I thee.*

Four years passed. No word from Richard. He was ever in her thoughts and in the very air she breathed. He was her first love, never to forget.

Don

Now, Nina was Don Marino's first love, never to forget. He came home from the service in World War II having experienced and lived through meeting the Russians in Berlin after crossing the ocean on the Queen Mary and then crossing the Rhine River in Germany, plus all the army combat against the enemy beforehand.

His Italian family of five brothers and five sisters, mother and father, greeted him warmly upon his return with ravioli that he could not eat—it was too rich after eating army food for so many years—and with wine that his father insisted he drink, but he could not—he never drank. Yet, it was a celebration; their son was home, as were four others.

Nina said, "Okay, I'll marry you," one day when she realized Don was her friend; she was very comfortable with him. He worshiped her, was very good to her, and would most probably be her soul mate for life. She gathered after much mind-searching, especially since Richard said a good-bye that she felt was forever, that Don meant sincerity and security.

Yet, if Richard had been in the church on her wedding day, she would have run out the door wearing her white wedding dress, not caring that it was snowing and very cold that February day.

It is now fifty years later, and Nina and Don are still together. Richard married Ann and had three children, yet his first love invades his thoughts often. He wonders what went wrong, blaming his shyness in his young years.

DARIA

Last but not least is Daria, beautiful Daria with the big smile showing off her perfect teeth, the mean sister who was so ashamed of her heritage and her Russian family who at one time lived near the dumps in Lily, Indiana. She longed to belong to an elite, well-bred, well-educated American family instead of having parents who spoke with a foreign accent and whose eating habits were not up to her high-falutin expectations.

Two years in Los Angeles, California, working in an insurance office doing office work, living in a boarding house with forty single women with no chance of ever being discovered for the movies, made Daria homesick for family—believe it or not.

She made an attempt at modeling, but she was only five-foot-four, not tall enough, and she was asked to undress and reveal her bare body; she refused when she saw the lust in the eyes of the photographer. Well, the disappointment made her conclude the hell with the glamorous life she had anticipated; it was sinful.

Daria had had her share of disappointments. Her first love, named John, went off to the priesthood when his father lost his life accidentally falling into a boiling vat of molten steel in the mill where he worked. His mother said it was an omen; her son must be a Jesuit priest. He obeyed his mother's command upon graduation from high school, even after having fallen in love with Daria and she with him.

Daria was left to cry for many years about the loss forever of her first love when he came to mind.

Her next love was the eldest son of a Slovak family, another boy named John who also was commanded to the priesthood, being the eldest son. More tears for Daria. John—a good name for a priest who may one day become pope. John would be a bell-ringer name to behold.

You would think that's enough. Oh no, yet a third love lost. Peter, the young man at Vera and Frank's wedding, was in love with Daria. The young man Sonny, her brother, was named after. His stepmother was a devout Catholic, never missing church services and seriously living in the shadow of God and all His laws. She proclaimed that Peter enter the priesthood.

Well, Peter did not agree and said he would run away and they would never see him again if he could not finish school, where Daria also attended—he was truly in love.

The stepmother finally complied.

After graduation, he joined the navy. World War II had begun when the Japanese attacked Pearl Harbor.

He found Daria in California a year and a half after she was there and asked her to marry him. Peter was stationed in San Francisco serving in the naval intelligence and was on leave. Daria flew from Los Angeles to see him when he pressured her to join him, remembering she loved him from early childhood.

In all their intimate conversations she learned he wanted many children, but Daria learned she could not have any—uncorrectable female problems.

She once again sacrificed a love, knowing she could never make him happy.

A year later she went home to Winsome, Indiana, to marry a man thirteen years her senior who cared not to have children.

They had known each other back home through friends of friends. He took a trip to California and looked her up, having remembered how beautiful she was.

They returned home together to be one. Bill and Daria made a beautiful couple.

The many years' difference in their ages made family members wonder what would happen to their marriage in their later years, when she still looked young and he old, with his friends looking the same.

Would they be together to the end as they both declared in the marriage ceremony?

Daria had too many memories of past loves that she could not have and wondered many times, especially when she had been made sentimental by too many drinks and was listening to her favorite recording of *Doctor Zhivago* to add to her illusions, what her life would have been like had she been able to marry so-and-so, or so-and-so, or yet another so-and-so. What then? Would he have kissed her more, hugged her more, been more romantic? Her Russian genes craved fulfillment of a deep love that she longed for in the depth of her being since discovering her first love, John Biatak, the priest, forever lost to her heart. Add another John and then Peter to her list of loves lost—so painful—so sad.

Her husband, Bill, was content to grow old gracefully while Daria longed for more, due to dwelling on the hurtful past. How tragic. How sad. Unfulfilled love. Settling for fourth best, yet she loved him.

They had no children to leave their lifelong possessions to or to grieve over them when gone. The only available lost love in her later years was Peter, who married another, had four children, then divorced and was free. Daria couldn't help but wonder if she would outlive her Bill and be available to once again nurture the love she had had at one time for Peter, the young man she fell in love with at her sister Vera's wedding when she was eight years old.

They made their home in Michigan where her handsome husband worked. He had gone on the bum during the Depression years, found work on the railroad, was forever grateful to the company, and stayed with them until retirement.

Having no friends or family in Michigan, in time Daria got lonesome for home. They moved back to Winsome when the company Bill worked for was able to transfer him to the area. Bill's family was close by. They visited them now and then and they visited Vera, her older sister, a great deal—after all, Daria had lived with her and her family for many years.

Daria continued being ashamed of her old-country mother, insisting she always dress up before coming to visit her. My God! What would the neighbors think if she was seen wearing bobby socks or rolled-down long stockings to the knees or a plain housedress? Oh, and heaven forbid, a *babushka!* Bill had to dress up just to cut the grass.

What was it about her that made her want to impress strangers who probably could not have cared less? They too probably had parents who came from the old country and had the same custom and manner of dress. But Daria lived in constant fear that everyone would find out about her poor foreign heritage, when she desperately wished all her life that she was upper class and did not knowingly have a family who lived near the dumps in Lily, Indiana.

She lived a lie in the desire to better herself at the risk of never acknowledging her family of a brother, sisters, and mother and father.

Mealtime meant silence at her parents' home when she was young, due to Alex's method of alleviating children's antics at the table, just as was the method in his home in Russia. If anyone spoke, a spoon hit his or her forehead to cease speech. This silence was overpowered by the sound of Alex as he slurped his food, especially soup. His eyebrows went up with each intake of the hot liquid he so enjoyed, having lived in Russia and not always had hot sustenance.

Well, Daria could not bear this practice and irritating sound to the point where she one time swore, dropped her spoon with a clatter, and left the table, only to be hit with the razor strap. That lead her to the decision of leaving home.

This irritation followed her throughout her life. She insisted that her husband not make any sound during meals, not even to let the silverware make a sound against the china. She would be so upset to experience this that it would bring on a headache.

She insisted on proper manners at all times and was thoroughly disgusted if all persons did not adhere to the sensitivities that made her almost jump out of her skin.

One time, Butter's daughter Beverly and her two children went to visit Daria. They parked their old rattle-trap of a car in Daria's driveway. Upon leaving they were asked not to park in the driveway again but to leave the old car in the street. Beverly easily deduced that Daria didn't want the neighbors to know she knew someone who drove an old junk of a car.

Highfalutin, puttin' on the Ritz, nose up in the air, hospital-clean Daria—she spent all of her living days striving to be above her family who lived at one time where they did.

When Beverly and her children drove off, they blew the car horn repeatedly, and with the windows of the car open, they waved and shouted as loudly as they could, "Bye, Aunt Daria," over and over again to arouse the neighbors. They never again went to visit their Aunt Daria—the bitch!

She served snacks to the children in the basement to avoid crumbs in the kitchen upstairs.

An African violet plant that Beverly brought as a gift had a bug on it. Well, Daria nearly had a heart attack; she still had an aversion to bugs.

No one in Daria's family knew where her husband worked; the job was too lowly to mention, according to his wife. She replied when asked, "Oh, he is in the electrical department of a big company." The truth, that he repaired railroad crossing gates, the family learned some years later when Bill drank three scotch and waters and couldn't give a damn what Daria thought. He was proud to have been given a job in the Depression years when people were hungry and homeless.

Bill was a great guy, very handsome, wore tailor-made suits, was impeccable in his dress, and never had anything bad to say about anyone. Everyone liked Bill. He was beautiful.

He played basketball for the state of Michigan and was quite a star, keeping up his physique as he was accustomed, yet he never bragged about his achievements in the sport he loved. His very private scrapbook was filled with newspaper articles that glorified his triumphs.

It wasn't long before Daria had rifts with her sisters, especially Vera, whom she visited too often, and decided to move to Florida when her husband retired from his job, where no one knew them or her family. She was thinking she would finally be happy with her secrets.

This is where she died just before her seventieth birthday, naming Nina, of all people, executor of her estate, knowing she and Don would take care of Bill, who was now eighty-two years old. He packed up, home and furnishings sold, and went to live in California. He lived quietly, enjoying the climate, his cigars that he smoked outdoors only, and Nina's good cooking.

The only time Daria's name was mentioned in the eight months he lived with them until he died was when Nina remarked one day, "Daria was a good cook too." Bill agreed, saying, "Yes. She was."

He had gained ten pounds during his short stay because his wife was sick for a long time and could not cook; she really had been a great cook.

In Daria's wallet Nina found a newspaper clipping announcing the ordination to the Jesuit priesthood of John Biatak, her first love of fifty-two years before. The news clipping with photo was yellow with age.

First loves are special, cherished by the heart till the end of time. Life—to open one's eyes each breaking day and breathe the air that enables us to feel small joys and perhaps see the sadness in other faces, bringing to light the knowledge that you may not be the only one in the world who has lost a first love.

In a bank vault in Florida was a sealed envelope that had "Daria's Life" written on it. Nina placed it in her purse, then transferred it into her carry-on bag to read on the plane trip home to California. But Bill sat on one side of her and Don on the other, and she didn't want Bill to read its contents, thinking Daria most certainly named her previous lost loves in the letter.

Nina wished to spare Bill being hurt; it was bad

enough he had just lost his wife and was uprooted from his home of many years.

Had she known then that Bill was almost blind (cataracts and glaucoma) and would never have been able to read the letter had Nina opened it, she could have read it on the plane as planned.

Instead, when they got home, they were so busy unpacking Bill's belongings and making him comfortable that she placed the letter in hiding until she could find the time to read it in seclusion and has as yet not found it—never to know "Daria's Life."

Should she find her letter, Peter will be the first to be advised (he knew of its existence). He is most anxious to know what she had to say after so many years; she was his first love, never to forget.

Daria and Peter were so much in love that their exchange of passion made it natural to go all the way and enjoy their intertwined bodies—this is what you do when in love.

When her husband, Bill, questioned her, knowing how she felt about Peter at one time, she denied, denied, denied, as was expected. Yet she thought everyone knew, because it was written on her face every time his name was mentioned—Peter, the boy who fell in love when he was eight. But Nina did not write this in her book.

This was Daria's secret, and only the lost letter would tell all. She died at the age of sixty-nine, a most unhappy soul who never achieved her goals; who knows what they were.

Peter died in his sleep with secrets in his heart.

Nina had none—it's all here.